MW01532993

Dead Man's Plan

Lee A. Eide

Copyright © 2009 by Lee A. Eide.

ISBN: Softcover   978-1-4415-2321-1

All rights reserved. No part of this book may be reproduced or transmitted in any form
or by any means, electronic or mechanical, including photocopying, recording, or by
any information storage and retrieval system, without permission in writing from the
copyright owner.

This is a work of fiction. Names, characters, places and incidents either are the product
of the author's imagination or are used fictitiously, and any resemblance to any actual
persons, living or dead, events, or locales is entirely coincidental.

This book was printed in the United States of America.

To order additional copies of this book, contact:
Xlibris Corporation
1-888-795-4274
www.Xlibris.com
Orders@Xlibris.com
60704

Dead Man's Plan

Mr. Barreiro,

You will be pleased to know that my book contains no references to or depictions of triple-wide baby strollers, Carl Gerbschmidt or #4 of Green Bay Packer fame. It is about a normal, down-to-earth guy who's courageous enough to make some extremely brave, difficult decisions that put him in extraordinary situations.

I love your show but then again, I like The Common Man's show too. BTW: I'm the one who gave Common the, "Red Sox, dead. Washed with the white sox and turned pink" bit. Anyway, I hope you enjoy the book. I'm available for interviews to discuss my book and my recovery from my wife's death in 2006

Take care - keep up the stellar work.

Lee A. Eide

CHAPTER ONE

Ricky Mann, a cell phone plastered to his ear like it was a giant plastic leech, walked along the edge of the horse-shaped swimming pool that dominated the back yard of his northern California estate. Riding the wave of success from four consecutive top ten movies, Ricky's name and likeness were splashed across pages in more entertainment publications than any other actor around. Along with fame, like dust kicked up from a Mustang flying over a dirt road, came the money. He d had this pool built eighteen months ago. As he made his way along the bottom side the 500-foot long structure—his name was written in black letters on the bottom—Ricky alternated between speaking and swigging a bottle of Michelob.

"She quit? Why in the hell for?"

Ricky squinted into the sun as it dropped toward the western horizon.

"Whaddya mean, I can't afford a maid? I'm a god damn star! I should be able to blow a few bucks here and there. It's your job to manage all this money. If you can't do it, there's plenty of people out there who'd jump at the chance."

Turning the corner, he started up the side of the pool. The horse's snout, along with the giant N in MANN, stared back at him. He chugged another fourth of the beer while half-listening to his agent, Jim Morton, detail the herd of expenses that had trampled over the actor's checking account over the last year and a half. Besides the $250,000 pool, Ricky had snapped up a Dodge Stealth, built onto his mansion, joined the San Diego Country Club, and thrown five lavishly furnished parties. Taken along with the perpetual purchases of new clothes, unending supply of alcohol and frequent illegal drug purchases—mostly coke or acid but Ricky never told Jim about that—it left the hot young star's savings as dry as the air just before a dust storm's approach.

"The money from the new movie deal will be coming in soon, right?"

Ricky threw back another slug of Michelob as he approached the top of the pool's head.

"Next month!? What the hell is the hold-up? That studio executive, president, vice-president, whatever the fuck he was, told me I'd get it by next week at the latest. You have to talk to them and get this straightened out. I'm not waiting another month for the damn money. I signed a contract, for Christ's sake. If they want me to do the fucking movie, they have to pay me. If they don't pay me within two weeks, we'll sue 'em. I'll find another movie to do."

Ricky threw back the rest of the beer, grimaced slightly, and then was about to set the empty down by the pool when he remembered he didn't have a maid to pick up after him. He spat out a string of profanities before deciding he'd have to haul the empty back inside the house.

"Not that easy? I don't give a rip if it's easy or not! If they can't pay me when they're supposed to, I'll find someone who can."

Ricky rounded the corner by the horse's backside as he listened to his agent and financial adviser preach about the value of budgeting.

"Yeah, yeah, yeah. I'll do it sometime," he said while waving off the idea. "Numbers are your job. You've got to find ways to make them come out right. Speakin' of numbers, how's the Dying Tree deal look?"

He stepped into the dining room and took a hard left. On his way to the refrigerator in the adjoining kitchen, Ricky rolled his eyes while using thumb and fingers from his right hand to simulate opening and closing lips. After throwing open the door, he grabbed another Michelob. Ricky strode over and plopped himself into a wood-backed chair at a table made of glass and wrought iron.

"Cut to the chase, Jim. Can I afford to do the deal or not? No, let me rephrase: How can we arrange to do the deal?"

Ricky twisted off the bottle cap during his agent's explanation. He tilted the amber bottle to his lips, closed his eyes and drunk it in like a he was a dying man in the desert who'd stumbled across a secret well of spring water.

"Other investors!? What the hell happened to using funds from Ricky Mann Productions to finance it?"

The actor hoisted both bare feet onto the table while leaning the chair's rear legs back. He began peeling the label off the bottle while listening to Jim Morton's answer.

"I took out how much for personal use?" Ricky yelled while jerking his feet off the wrought iron table. He slammed the beer on the table so hard the foam rose up and overflowed onto and between the iron grid work.

"God damn mother fucker," he muttered, then said, "Fax me my bank account statements for the last year. I gotta see for myself. No, wait. Never fucking mind. I'll take your word for it. Just find other investors if you need to. I don't care how you do it but take care of it!"

Ricky tore the phone from his ear and hurled it off the far wall of the dining room.

"And don't call back until you got some good news for me!" he yelled across the room.

He slugged down half the beer. Ricky stomped over the carpeting into the living room. A punch of the black remote brought the huge-screen TV to life. The movie star changed the channel to 32. "Entertainment Tonight" was on. He waited to see if there was any mention of his latest movie, "Massacre on the Prairie", the one Ricky was expecting payment from or he'd quit the project. They'd begun shooting it last week. Ten minutes produced nothing but reports on Sly Stallone, Arnold Schwartzenegger, Sharon Stone, and Harrison Ford.

"Get a fucking clue, would ya? Those guys are yesterday's news," he grumbled before sucking down more of the beer.

A quick visual tour of the immediate area featured heaps of dirty clothes, crumpled beer cans, four different celebrity gossip rags, and three days of newspapers.

"Gotta get another maid," he muttered while making his way into the dining room where he retrieved the thrown cell phone. He punched in CODE and one. The phone dialed the number of the nearest Domino's.

"I want a large deluxe pizza, thin crust, with extra cheese," he began. "How soon can you get it here?"

While listening to the woman's response, he idly tossed the empty bottle of Michelob on to the pile of old ones by the recliner.

"Thirty minutes? Don't you know who you're talking to, little girl? This is THE Ricky Mann. Get it here in fifteen minutes and there'll be nice big tip for you and the driver."

He powered the phone off before the woman had a chance to reply. Ricky burped long and loud, barely fighting back the urge to do his Barry White impression through the belch. He'd save that for another day.

"Ummm, now that's good beer," he announced. Ricky fell back into the recliner in front of the television set. He briefly considered throwing one of his old movies into the DVD player but blew off the idea. The pizza'd be here before long. He leaned back the chair, closed his eyes, and waited for the doorbell.

CHAPTER TWO

The town council meeting officially ended ten minutes ago. The other five members of Dying Tree's council—two men and three women—had left for home or wherever else they might be going on this muggy, clear South Dakota evening. Bob McCallum and Rosie Dale, both sporting blonde hair turning gray, sat across from each other at the long rectangle of simulated wood that had been privy to thirteen years of town council meetings. While Bob cheerfully accepted his transitional state of hair, Rosie fought back with dyes and wigs. Of course, Bob had been married to Kate for thirty-two years while Rosie had divorced last year.

Bob grimaced down the last few drops of cold coffee from a Styrofoam cup. Rosie smiled while sipping Evian.

"We can't go through with this," he began, "without more proof that Ricky has the financial backing to see this thing through to the end. I don't care how many top ten movies he's starred in over the years. You show me a famous movie star and I'll show you someone who will find ways to spend all that money. Most of the Hollywood types, not all, mind you, but most, aren't exactly wizards at saving money. Their egos and greed lead 'em around like a carrot in front of a horse."

"Or a bottle of beer in front of Jimmy Rowland," quipped Rosie.

Jimmy Rowland was the town drunk. He wasn't quite as old or rotund as Otis Campbell but toward the end of many a night of heavy vodka consumption, Jimmy's speech sure sounded like Otis'.

"I disagree with you, however, about Ricky's investors. With all his connections, I bet he knows plenty of folks who've got a small fortune stashed away. If he says he knows some people who will help fund the project, I believe him. After all, he was born and raised in Dying Tree. That's gotta count for something," said Rosie.

Bob shrugged, muttered something, and then strode over to the coffee pot for a refill. After pouring in nondairy creamer and stirring it in with his right index finger, he approached the table.

"It counts for something but you gotta remember a lot of things have happened to Ricky between grade school and Hollywood stardom. He may have developed a different way of looking at the world since he was playing third base for the Dying Tree boys team from McKinley Elementary School."

"Not our Ricky. He's just a good ol' boy at heart. You'll see."

"Does this mean you plan to vote for the city installing—at no charge—sewer and water lines, giving him fifteen acres of land, not making the business pay any real estate taxes for the first five years, and giving them a liquor license?" Bob said before slurping the fresh coffee.

"I haven't decided one way or the other yet but if I had to choose right now, I'd vote for granting them economic incentives."

"*Economic incentives*? You mean corporate welfare. And I'm sure, Miss Dale, that you're not allowing your old high school crush on Mr. Mann to cloud your judgment on this topic," Bob said while reaching for his coffee.

An exaggerated series of eyelash batting preceded her response.

"Whatever do you mean, sir? I, as a self-respecting lady of good reputation am above that sort of thing," Rose chimed in her best Southern belle tone, then shot him a serious look. "But honestly, that's not why I'm leaning toward going through with the project. This town needs a fresh addition, something that builds on Old West but at the same time adds something unique to the town. I know the economy sucks and we're already up to our collective eyeballs in gaming and bars—"

"That's 'saloons'," Bob corrected.

"I beg your pardon. I sit corrected: *saloons*. Anyway, I think it'd be great for the area if one of our own, who's become a down right national celebrity, returns home and builds something like this."

"I'd agree with you if he did it with his own money," Bob began, "but he's not satisfied with the city rolling out the red carpet for him. He wants Dying Tree to fit his new place with red carpeting, sewer and power lines, and even give him the damn land to put the red carpeting over."

"What? Putting carpeting over land? What are you talking about? I think you' added something pretty damn strong to that coffee," said Rosie.

"You know what I mean," he replied. "My point is Ricky expects the city to subsidize at least half the cost of the thing. With the condition of the state's economy what it is, and the political mood no better, we can't afford to be wrong about this."

"Compared with the state economy, Dying Tree is in great shape. Unemployment is just over four percent in our county compared to nine or ten percent for the state. Inflation is between one and two percent," she countered.

"The problem is the city of Dying Tree's budget has taken a beating the last two years. First we lose revenue from the tourist trade because of all the new casinos sprouting up across the state, then the referendum to build a new city hall goes through, which we desperately needed because the damn building is falling apart inside and out, so that's $300,000 out-of-pocket expenses for the city in just the first year of construction, and then last winter, Mother Nature, in her infinite wisdom, dumped the highest annual snowfall since the Depression on us. And of course, with the global recession getting worse every day, Dying Tree is dancing along the edge of a deep, deep canyon of debt. Right now, we're okay, but one financial misstep and . . ."

Bob stood up, leaned across the table and peered over the edge of it before saying, "Well, it's a long way down."

Rosie sipped her water, then said, "You sound like you know what you're talking about, Bob."

"It's nothing you didn't already know, I'm sure."

"But what if Ricky's entertainment complex turns out to be profitable?"

"Then thankfully we'll never know how deep the canyon is."

He knocked back the rest of the coffee, crumpled up the cup, and tossed it toward a wastebasket crouched in the corner of the room. It ricocheted off the left rim, struck the back right edge, then bounced neatly off the right-hand wall and disappeared into the bowels of the wastebasket.

"Never a doubt," Bob said.

"If you're that lucky, you should head on down to Frank's Poker Palace. This could be your lucky night."

"Nah, I think it's time to go home. I don't want to press my luck."

CHAPTER THREE

Lee Wyatt pushed through the front door and waited for five seconds. He shook his head, a rueful smile skipping across his face like the countless stones he and his brother had slung across ponds in their youth. For a few uncertain seconds, Lee was waiting for Frank, a St. Bernard puppy they'd had for six months. For a few seconds, he'd forgotten that they'd made the difficult decision to give the dog to another couple, someone who had a big enough yard to let it stay outside when they weren't home. When Lee and his wife Mary had it, the animal had driven them crazy by chewing up anything it could reach. Carpeting, shoes, toilet paper rolls, empty beer and pop cans, phone and television cords—they were all fair game for Frank. The dog's energy level, though certainly less than many breeds, was still sufficient to leave the animal bored and restless. Chewing was his way of passing the long, otherwise boring days while his owners were off at work.

Then the piles of dog poop began appearing. Frank had apparently just been completely housebroken when evidence to the contrary keep appearing with daily, stinking regularity. Mary wasn't going to put up with it and while Lee would normally have given the animal a chance to come around, it was painfully obvious Frank wasn't happy in their two-bedroom townhouse. From an emotional, recreational perspective, the dog was suffocating.

Lee shut the door. He shuffled to the table in the dining room, set the briefcase on top of the table, and said softly as he made for the refrigerator, "Sorry Franky, we tried to make it work. Hope you're happy in your new home."

The accountant pulled back the door, surveyed the artificially cooled landscape, and after careful deliberation, opted for a bottle of Bud.

The caller ID flashed an incessant blinking red light. Someone had called. Lee, with the beer in his left hand, used his right hand to work the buttons on the phone accessory. Mary had called at 5:03 p.m. She'd left a message.

He snapped up the portable phone, keyed in the message retrieval number, punched in the secret code, and listened to his wife's recorded voice.

"Hi, I'm out with a few girls from the office. I should home be home between ten and eleven. I'll call you later to let you know what's going on. Talk to you soon."

A female voice began giving him options about saving the message and so on. He hit the 1 and then the * button to end the call. Lee and his mass-marketed beer migrated to the patio. As soon as they were outside, a gold and white Persian cat, belly hanging about four inches above the floor, ambled after him.

"BROOOWWWW," yelled the cat as it approached him. Lee dropped on to the wrought iron bench they'd purchased earlier in the summer. He patted his lap.

"Come on up, big guy. You can do it."

Bellows took two more steps, paused, crouched, and launched its considerable girth into the air. Though the top paws reached its goal, the declawed state his owners had cursed him with meant it had no way to get a good grip to pull itself up. Anticipating such, Lee hoisted the rotund kitty up into his lap. A cloud of cat hairs danced in the air in front of him.

"Now was that so hard? Don't answer that question," Lee said scratching the animal under the chin. Bellows' eyes closed immediately as it rolled on to its back. He rubbed the exposed belly.

"BROOOWWW," gave way to passionate purring. The cat settled in for a short summer's nap.

As Lee watched two teen-age boys blast ground-strokes back and forth on the tennis court across the way from their unit, he thought back to the phone message. *Out with the girls* was her code for being with her newest boyfriend. Pete, Harry, Larry, he couldn't recall for sure. The particulars didn't matter. Mary was fast becoming a female Bill Clinton. Lee had thus far played along with the charade. She suspected he knew of the affairs but they'd never discussed it. Though they'd never separated, in an emotional sense, Mary was never really there for him. Maybe it was their different interests. Lee ate up spectator sports. She imbibed public television. He loved to play golf. She had no idea what a loft wedge was and didn't care to ever find out. He was good with numbers. She hadn't ever balanced her checking account. He was a regular church-goer at the Lutheran church five blocks away. She stepped inside churches only for the occasional wedding or funeral. He read novels like a madman. She watched television religiously.

Whatever the root causes, the result was a missed connection. Checking accounts weren't the only separate pieces in their lives. Their spirits had never really danced with one another. A nebulous but very real barrier had always kept them apart, the energy exchange between them limited and superficial.

What the hell were they supposed to do about it now? Nine years of marriage had produced no children, which was fine with him. The world had entirely too many folks the way it was. Lee reasoned that it was okay to have children but if you had them, your whole soul had to be devoted to loving and raising them in the very best way you knew how. Only the people who were truly enthused about having kids should have them. That was his philosophy. There was plenty of ways for non-child producing adults to help care for the world's children. Babysitting nieces, nephews and neighbor kids; donating to the March of Dimes and United Way; leading Boy Scout and Girl Scout troops; saying hi to your friends' children; behaving politely in public; and praying for the safety and well-being of children around the world at church services were just the tip of iceberg.

Lee swigged his beer and then watched the boys play tennis for a several minutes, his mind slowly blowing away mental cobwebs with each THWACK of the tennis ball. He glanced down. Bellows was snoozing fitfully, the stout feline struggling to slip into a deeper sleep. The beer was nearly gone. He decided to pace himself on the last quarter of the beer so that the feline got in a few more moments of sack time.

Having trudged through the marital muck of his life, he turned to his job. He'd labored for seven years as an Intermediate Accountant III at the Global Link Federal Credit Union in Richfield, Minnesota. Standing only fifteen miles from their town home, it was like the Mall of America—big, convenient, and profitable. But he'd grown increasingly dissatisfied with his role at the credit union. Whenever he'd applied for a higher position within the department, like accounting supervisor, he'd been rejected. Moreover, the pay at his mid-level accounting position was considerably below market. The company line was that the tremendous benefits made up for the lower pay.

While knocking off most of the rest of the beer, Lee considered that argument. While it was true the medical, retirement and almost-free flying benefits were significantly greater than the average employer, he knew the primary reason for the lower pay. It was the higher-than-normal compensation of executive management. At the expense of all the other employees, the higher-ups were overpaid. Lee'd seen memos and journal entries that detailed bonuses to the execs, usually over $150,000 for the three of them. While the president, CEO and CFO weren't making the exorbitant salaries you read about in Time or Newsweek or hear on the evening news, for the credit union industry, their management salaries were well above market. And that was before the year-end bonuses.

Lee slugged down the last few drops of Bud, smiled at the team of horses on the label, and then glanced down at Bellows. All four paws were in the air, shooting off at different angles. His spider web-fine whiskers twitched.

"Dreaming of a nice fat little mouse with a broken leg, huh?"

Then he thought, no, he's probably dreaming of a large sausage pizza with extra onions. The cat, like Frank, ate anything it could reach. He especially liked steak hot off the grill. One time Lee tried to retrieve a piece of steak the little shit had stolen off his plate. When he'd cornered the cat, it actually growled at him as Lee tried to recover the pilfered meat. Then it hit him. That's how he felt about his years at the credit union. What was rightfully his—in other words, fair pay for all the years of competent, loyal service—had been swiped off his plate by the voracious claws of upper management.

He'd been tolerant of the situation for all these years but while outwardly he didn't express much discontent, inwardly it'd been gnawing away at his emotional guts. Now, today, on this Friday night in June, Lee Wyatt decided that for once in his life, he was going to be one-hundred percent truthful with himself. No making excuses for people. He was going to see what the situation truly was, compare it to his feelings, and act wisely and truthfully. Number one, he was getting ripped off by the credit union brass. He wasn't going to put up with it any longer. It wasn't fair to him or his coworkers.

Number two, what could he do about it? If he told his boss, the controller, about it, it wouldn't do any good. Even if he went right to the top and told the president himself—John Roff—it wouldn't do any good. If Lee told him the rest of the non-management workers wanted a bigger slice of the financial pie, John Roff, acting as voice of the executives, would growl. But unlike Bellows, he wouldn't act so docile when Lee tried to actually take back what was rightfully his. If he filed a formal complaint with the board of directors of the credit union or even with the National Credit Union Administration, the growl would escalate to a bite.

Lee could easily envision John Roff and his cronies inventing an excuse to fire him. They'd go through the employee manual until they found an obscure rule that he'd broken. They'd use that as ammunition for firing his troublemaking ass.

He reached down and gently picked up Bellows. The cat muttered a cry of protest and resentment over being roused from its slumber.

"Sorry big guy, but you're separating me from another beer," he told Bellows before setting the feline on the bench. The cat hopped down and ambled back inside, just ahead of him.

He snapped up another beer and hauled it back outside. The two teen-age boys playing tennis were switching sides of the court. The taller one kidded the other about being behind. The teased one brushed off the taunt and said something about not losing another the game the rest of the match.

Lee returned to his spot on the wrought iron bench. He twisted off the top and tilted the bottle to his mouth. After a long sigh, he gently laid the container down on a near-by stand. His mind slipped back into the house of thought he'd just been in a few minutes earlier. No, it was true that there was really nothing he could to improve his standing at the credit union. Executive management was entrenched there, meaning sub-par pay for the rest of the employees wouldn't improve much. That meant he'd have to find an accounting position at a different organization.

He shook his head. The prospect of staying in the numbers game didn't exactly excite him. It didn't, as Jimmy Dean would say about a certain brand of sausage, melt his butter. Lee knew accounting was a critical part of any business. It was just that he didn't want to have to personally do it any longer. There were plenty of other qualified accountants in the universe. If Lee Allen Wyatt hung up his ten-key calculator and pocket protector, the accounting industry wouldn't be any worse off. The pool of accountants and bookkeepers was plenty big enough to absorb the loss, especially given the depressed economy.

The challenge was finding something he wanted to do for a living. No easy, obvious answer popped up to replace the void left by accounting's exit.

What the hell, there's gotta be an answer, he thought. Then he realized what he needed to do was completely change his thinking process. He had to somehow dig down deep inside to find his true self. That meant not being duped by surface appearances and past behaviors. He couldn't rely on those outward, easy clues for answers. He had to reinvent himself by changing his inner landscape. To do that, he had to change his outer landscape as well. His current life was too full of routines and structures pointing to his old, unhappy, out-of-place self. To induce a drastic change in his attitude, Lee felt he had to drastically alter his outer environment.

"You gotta get the hell out of Dodge, partner," he muttered. The now ex-accountant slugged down the rest of the beer, grimaced, sighed, and belched.

"Enough of that shit for awhile," he declared before marching upstairs. On the way up, he petted Bellows, told the cat good-bye, and then filled a suitcase with clothes and several paperback books. On his way toward the front door, he paused long enough to slip the wedding band off his finger and leave it on the dining room table. He considered leaving a long, detailed, emotional note for Mary. Instead he scribbled on a Post-It note, "Like Dennis Miller used to say, I AM OUTTA HERE. We're finished. We'll work out details of the divorce later. Right now, I've got to go."

From there he hustled into the living room. He found a photograph of Bellows in an album, pulled it out and slipped it into the suitcase. One last look around. Nope, nothing else he really had to have.

"Oh what the hell, might as well finish off the rest of them," he said before opening the fridge to grab the last four Buds. "Now I'm outta here."

He walked through the house, out through the front door, and into the garage. Two minutes later, the maroon Escort rumbled out of sight.

*　　*　　*

He'd been driving over six hundred miles, three-quarters of it on I-90. It was a little before five o'clock in the morning. Lee had seen a billboard and two highway signs about the Badlands National Park exit. It'd be coming up pretty damn soon. As a child of six or seven, he'd visited the badlands in North Dakota. They were, as he recalled, just outside a small town named Medora. He'd never been to the badlands in South Dakota. One thing was for sure: he was sick to death of driving along the flat prairie land at 85 mph. The sheer monotony of the landscape, drone of the Escort's engine, and consumption of the beer conspired together. Their ultimate aim was, of course, to make him fall asleep behind the wheel. Though he injected three cups of coffee into his fatigued system, the tricky trio of boring landscape, beer and engine noise were winning the battle. Teetering on the precipice of sleep, Lee determined he had to either pull off the road and give in to the siren song of slumber or take a detour through the Badlands National Park. Eager to put as much distance between his old life and himself as possible, he opted for the second choice.

The sky grew lighter but sunrise was still another hour away. As he eased the old Escort up to the guard's station at the park's entrance, ominous sounds drifted from under the hood. Loud, clicking, abnormal sounds that seemed to his admittedly mechanically-challenged ears to be cries for help. Like a loved one sitting by a terminally ill loved one, there was nothing to do but pray and assure the patient that they'd be all right.

"Just one in the car, sir?" asked a clean-cut, young man of perhaps twenty-two or twenty-three.

"Yep."

"Ten dollars, please."

"Ten dollars?!"

"Yes sir. It's ten dollars per person. Didn't you see the rates on the sign back there?" he asked.

"Oh, is that what that was?"

A nod of the head.

"That's right. You look pretty tired. You know, there's a Super Eight right off the interstate. It's only another five miles ahead. I'll be happy to give them a call to see if they've got a room available."

"That's all right. I'll be fine. Just another cup or eight of this—" Lee raised the plastic mug of coffee from Tom Thumb "and I'll be fine."

"If you say so, sir. Now then, that'll be ten dollars. We also accept Visa and MasterCard if you don't have the cash."

"Let me see, hold on a second or two. I think I've got a ten here," Lee said while rifling through his pants pockets in search of his wallet.

"Aha, here we go."

Lee handed over the bill. The park employee thanked him and urged him to pull over and take a nap at one of the scenic lookouts if he needed to.

"Thanks. If I need to, I will."

He waved at the young man before shifting into drive. The Escort groaned, hesitated, and then grudgingly eased ahead. Lee began to reach toward the glove compartment for the maintenance log. He wanted to see when the date of the last oil change and tune-up.

"Fuck it," he said. At this point, it didn't matter. Checking the maintenance log now would be like a doctor asking a patient stricken with the Ebola virus when they'd last had a physical. His old Ford Escort, which had taken him many places during the last eight years, including well over a hundred golf courses, to and from work over interstate and city roads, out to the Grand Canyon on one vacation (1993) and over to Fenway Park (1996) on another, would carry him as far as it could. And that was that. Like most people and even most animals, it did the best it could and the cards of chance would come up as it they did.

"Come on, baby," he whispered soothingly, "you can do it. Daddy wants a new life. You be a good girl and keep going, and you can sleep all day and maybe even part of the night after we reach Wall."

Wall was home to Wall Drug, an urban legend for the millions of folks who'd never been there. Of course, millions of people had trekked through the Dakota prairie over the seventy plus years since the business had opened up in the early 1930's. The advertising signs along Interstate 90 for Wall Drug were as numerous as Wilt Chamberlain's one-night stands. WHERE IN THE HELL IS WALL DRUG was plastered to thousands, probably millions, of car bumpers. WHERE IN THE HECK IS WALL DRUG was available to the folks with aversions to profanity.

As he eased the car around the hairpin curves, Lee marveled at the bizarre landscape. The Badlands were just behind the Mt. Rushmore and Crazy Horse monuments as South Dakota tourist attractions. He could certainly understand why. The terrain was so diametrically opposed to most of the state. Instead of the wind-whipped flatlands, the topography looked like God had dropped several hits of acid and went to town. In reality, it'd taken wind and water millions of years to create the mazes of twisted, turning, nonsensically shaped hills, canyons and mounds that spread out before him. The variety of shapes and angles was staggering. Most people said they saw shapes like castle towers and battlements, church spires and pyramids. It reminded Lee of gazing up at the sky as child and trying to identify what the clouds looked like. To his left, he saw a jumble of mini-hills that's pattern of peaks approximated the big dipper.

To his left, the sun hurled red javelins of fire from 93 million miles away. Most of the land was tucked snugly in blankets of shadow, still snoozing happily. That'd change soon enough but for now, the lunar-like expanse of land was more dark than light, the jambalaya of configurations hiding more than it flaunted. He braked, the old Escort's speedometer down to twenty miles an hour, as he and his old friend negotiated another tight curve.

After the road straightened out, Lee leaned on the accelerator. The speedometer remained at twenty mph, however. He frowned, then applied more pressure on the gas pedal. The Escort's insides growled and shrieked but wouldn't speed up for him.

"Shit," he muttered. "Come on, girl, you can do it. We're all pulling for you."

We was God and himself. And maybe the security guard he'd just spoken to. As for the rest of the world, it probably didn't give a shit. There were bigger fish to be concerned with. Pockets of abject poverty, the disintegration of the family, collapse of ethics in government leaders, ruination of natural resources, especially the waters of the planet, and so on. But for Lee Wyatt, the biggest fish in his pond was his dying auto-mo-fucking-bile. He still didn't know exactly where he wanted to end up but he knew it wasn't here. Not in middle of the Badlands National Park near Wall, South Dakota.

"See, I'm going nice and slow now. I'm not standing on the accelerator any more. Doesn't that feel better?" he purred to the car.

His old buddy responded by losing even more speed while issuing a series of unhealthy sounds from underneath the hood.

Fifteen mph.

He glanced in the rearview mirror. There was no one behind him. That was good.

Ten mph.

"God damn it."

Five mph.

Grudgingly, he pointed the car at the turnoff for a scenic overlook. The motor died before he was all the way off the road. The car's rear end stuck out in the westbound lane, blocking a quarter of the road.

"Oh come on, you could have least made it another thirty feet, for Christ's sake."

He slammed his fists off the steering wheel.

"Oh well, life rips your heart out and then you die a horrible, slow, agonizing death. What can you do?"

He sat in the driver's seat. He'd never before seen and heard a car die. The odometer froze on 99,892 and one-tenth miles. Lee briefly thought about turning the key again to see what would happen.

"Not a chance in hell," he announced, then did it anyway.

If ever a car cried, the sound issuing from under its hood was it. It sounded like the dying cry of a cat or dog that'd been fatally struck by a car. His friend the car was road kill, though the terminator wasn't another car but rather time itself.

Lee breathed out a heavy sigh, then said reverentially, "Thanks for the memories, old girl."

The ex-accountant laid his head on the steering wheel, closing his eyes for several seconds. As tired as he was, Lee knew if he didn't move within five or ten seconds, he'd be asleep at the wheel. His eyes snapped open. The desolate, bizarre beauty of the Badlands surrounded him, the sheer weirdness of the misshapen topography evidence of forces much greater than but not necessarily adverse to himself. He tried unsuccessfully to identify the row of shapes standing off to his right and fifty yards ahead. One instant they appeared to be a row of headstones, complete with engravings summarizing the lives of the persons buried several feet under, the next they were giant dominoes with sidebars about the games they'd been involved in over the years. Lee shook his head in an attempt to connect with the reality of the situation. Now the row had been transformed into a line of statues of well-known presidents of the United States with summaries of the secrets of their lives. Little-known facts such as childhood acts of theft, sexual fantasies or heretofore unknown interests like woodcarving or poker replaced normal presidential fact sheets.

Without realizing why he was doing it or how quickly he was truly moving, Lee strode toward the shapes in question. A burning desire to know just what in the hell those things really were pulled him relentlessly closer as a breathless young female virgin draws her boyfriend closer by undoing the top buttons of her shirt.

Five feet away, Lee decided it wasn't quite close enough to identify the true nature of the shapes. The first two strides were without incident but the third one was, unbeknownst to the strider, too close to the hill's edge. Before he could do anything about it, Lee was tumbling and bouncing down a sharp incline. Though he threw up both hands, the series of collisions with the hard clay sand rocked him like waves attacking the Titanic. The last one tugged him under. Darkness was complete and absolute.

He woke an indeterminate time later. Though exhausted, he started climbing up the incline. Details of the valley from which he climbed were fogged with fatigue and shadow. Forty, perhaps fifty steps later, he reached the top. The steepness of the climb surprised him as his breathing grew increasingly difficult during the ascent. After reaching relatively flat land again, he bent over to rest. Maybe thirty seconds later, he was ready to continue. Lee shuffled over to his fallen car, undid the straps on the carrier, and grabbed the 18-speed bike. He nearly toppled over after hopping on but righted himself just in time. After he'd fallen back into the routine of pedaling and balancing, Lee grew exuberant of his successful negotiation of the highway. A crazy smile shot onto his face. Though the number of reasons for his happiness were no doubt multiple and complex, his consciousness soared above them all, slave to no one explanation but thankful to whatever kept him going along this lonely highway He swung a glance over his left shoulder and then waved one last time at the silent, still 1981 Ford Escort.

CHAPTER FOUR

"I'm just a poor old South Dakota boy who helped his papa grow some corn and soybeans," began Mayor Ralph Tergis, a man so skinny except for a slight beer belly that he could have stepped in for a scarecrow on vacation. "You wanna tell us just exactly what all those numbers mean?"

The six city council members looking at the figures—the mayor wasn't on the council but frequently sat in on the meetings, especially important ones with hot issues—wore expressions of confusion that let Ralph know his question was not only justified but necessary.

Bob McCallum, who'd been so wrapped up with creating the intricate maze of figures, now appeared puzzled and maybe even a little hurt by the question. But after stepping back from the blackboard to study what'd he created, he chuckled while shaking his head.

"Well I'll be dipped in—"

"Bob!" chimed in Agatha Hines, an 80-year-old retired grade school and current Sunday school teacher at Mount Olivet Lutheran Church.

"A big old pile of vanilla ice cream," he finished while staring directly at Mrs. Hines.

"All right, Mayor, I see your point. Maybe I did go little overboard with the numbers and such. My point is that if we grant the state's most favored son all the concessions he's asking for and the town pays for sixty percent of the cost of the casino-based entertainment complex, and the thing doesn't bring in a whole flock of people into Dying Tree to spend their money at the tourist trade, the city will be broke. We're hurting' now because of the global recession, the half-million we've spent on the new city hall, which we gotta have, don't get me wrong, and the fall off in monies from sales tax which is, of course, due to less tourism because every town in the area seems to have a damned—"

"Bob McCallum, we would all appreciate it if you could speak with a civil, Christian tongue," Mrs. Hines said.

"I'm sorry, Mrs. Hines. Okay, every town in the area seems to have a darned video slot machine in every business in the stinking town.

"'Bout the only places that don't have one are funeral parlors and they've probably got plans to start installing them soon. Anyway, the bottom line is I don't think the city of Dying Tree is in any position to be giving away anything right now, even to a native who's turned into a movie star like Ricky Mann."

"But shouldn't a casino and golf course with Ricky's name attached to it be a gold mine?"

It was Ron Deere, the owner of Ron's General Store. He'd seen every one of Ricky's movies at least twice and owned videos of all the movies on video.

"Probably," Bob McCallum granted, "but that assumes there's enough other financing out there to build a quality facility. The town of Dying Tree can do only so much. A big chunk of the money has to come from Ricky and his fellow investors. I have yet to see anything that proves Ricky Mann can afford this type of investment."

"I heard he made twenty-five million dollars last year," said Ron Deere.

"That may well be but what you make is only half the equation. If you make a hundred million and spend a hundred and fifty million, whaddya got left?" countered Bob McCallum, a rueful smile splayed across his facial terrain.

The rest of the town council sat there, deep in thought. Occasionally one would cast a look at the figures strewn across the blackboard. A couple of them jotted something on the printed agenda they'd each received before the meeting began. Mayor Ralph Tergis doodled on his copy. He found it helped him think more clearly. After several seconds, he folded tan, baseball bat-sized arms across his chest. Using his right foot, he pushed away from the table.

"Seems to me, we oughta get a financial statement from old Ricky Mann," he declared.

"And do a credit report," said Bob.

"What do the rest of you all think?" asked Rosie Dale.

Nods of the head and murmured "yeahs" peppered the air.

"All right, we're agreed then. Before we give anything to Ricky Mann, we obtain those two documents. Then we study them and act accordingly," said Bob. "You want to contact Ricky's agent to see if he'll give us a statement of his financial worth," he said to the mayor. Ralph nodded.

"Good. I'll have Nate down at the bank run a credit report for us," he said.

"Is there any other business anyone wants to bring up?" Bob asked.

After a brief bout of silence, he declared, "Meeting's adjourned."

*　　*　　*

Eileen Eide frowned at the flashing lights ahead. Two trucks and a blue bike were cornered by a black and white police car, one of the three owned by the Dying Tree Police Department. Joel Meyers had the day shift so he got the pleasure of investigating the accident.

Eileen recognized the drivers of the two trucks and one car but she couldn't identify the fourth man there. While she wondered who he was, her gaze crept over a bicycle laying on the shoulder of the road, sprawled fifty yards behind the congregation of men. The bike didn't look damaged and the fourth man, who must have been the rider of the bicycle, didn't appear to be seriously injured. The area was free of blood and he was standing up so presumably he'd suffered no broken bones from the mishap.

" . . . damn bike swerved out in the middle of the damn lane. Nothin' I could do but slam on the brakes," said Nate Anderson

"You coulda swerved, for Chrissake," yelled Norm Turner, his green eyes almost glowing with anger.

"If you wouldn't have been ridin' my ass, which is a course illegal as hell, you woulda had time to stop before rear endin' me," shot back Nate. "That's the trouble with you, Norm. You're always in so damn much of a hurry that you just can't stand if someone else isn't drivin' like as fast as you are, which is always at least ten miles an hour over the speed limit."

"As usual, you're exaggerating like hell," said Norm. "Just like the time you said you hit a drive three-hundred yards on the 17th hole of that tournament we had a few years back—"

"Pipe down, both of you!" said Officer Meyers as he dug out the official report form. He grabbed a pen that had been clipped to a shirt pocket, licked the tip of it, and said, "All right you two, you can both shut up while I get this guy's side of the story. All right, first of all, what's your name?"

"Lee Wyatt."

"Where you from?"

"The Twin Cities, Bloomington, to be exact. It's about twenty miles south of Minneapolis," said the stranger.

"And you rode your bicycle all the way from there?" asked Office Meyers, eyebrows raised.

"Nope. Just from the Badlands to here," he said.

"That's still 'bout a hundred and thirty miles," remarked the policeman. "You ridin' for charity or somethin'?"

"Nope. It's a long story. I, ah, well, I just had to get out of that place."

"What are you, runnin' from the police back in Minnesota? You can be honest with me, son."

Lee laughed.

"Oh no, it's nothing like that," he began, "I haven't done anything illegal. It's just that my situation at home and at work was no longer palatable. I had to have a change of scenery to salvage my life. After hopping in my car, for some reason or maybe for no reason at all, I headed for Rochester, which is about an hour south of the Cities. When I saw the signs for I-90, I decided that was the road I needed to be on. After reaching it, I just kept going west on the interstate. Then my car broke down right after entering the Badlands National Park. Since I wasn't in the mood to wait for a tow truck and I didn't think the old wreck was worth repairing anyway, I hopped on my 18-speed bike and took off. That was two and a half days ago."

"Why'd you swerve? You on something?" asked Meyers.

"Hey, feel free to do a BreathAlyzer or any kind of drug test you want. I'm clean. I was just feeling tired and a little light-headed from the heat and lack of food. I haven't eaten much the last few days."

Officer Meyers studied him for several seconds before saying, "Are you passing through our fair city or planning to stay for awhile?"

Lee met the policeman's gaze, shot a glance at the town down below and then tilted his head up so he could see the sky. After a few seconds, his gaze reunited with Officer Meyer's.

"I think I'm going to stay for awhile," he said.

"The Prairie View Palace is a clean, quiet, fairly-priced place to stay," said the policeman. "Or there's the Saddle Creek Inn on Main Street. Little more expensive but they have a real nice, big swimming pool and Jacuzzi."

"I'm looking for just about the cheapest place I can find that doesn't have any cockroaches or psycho owners," Lee replied. "I'd also like to find temporary employment if possible."

"Well I can't help you with that. As far as this here accident goes, it's the responsibility of the operators of motor vehicles to be aware of and be prepared to react appropriately to any traffic. It doesn't matter whether it's cars, trucks, semis, motorcycles, farm equipment, pedestrians, or bicycles.

Drivers are expected, by the laws of the land, to be prepared to react to movements by vehicles or pedestrians in the area. While it is true bicyclists, like any slower moving traffic, are to keep to the right, it's still the duty of drivers to react appropriately if the slower moving traffic isn't all the way over to the right. Since bicycles have no protection against collisions with cars, it's the responsibility of the automobile operators to avoid bicyclists if a collision appears likely."

"What about the driver's responsibility to the cars behind him?" demanded Norm.

Meyers smiled while shaking his head.

"Norm, you know what the law is. Any rear ending accident is presumed to be the fault of the driver in back. That's common knowledge. Least it should be."

"That mean you're givin' me a ticket?" he asked.

Office Meyers eyed Norm, cast a glance at the damage to Nate's truck, which was minimal, and sighed.

"No, not this time. You two fellas just exchange insurance information and we can all be on our way. Mr. Wyatt, I can, if you like, give you and your bike there a lift to one of the hotels I mentioned."

"Hold on there," chimed in Eileen Eide.

All heads snapped toward her.

"Eileen, you sneaky little son of gun, what the heck are you talkin' about?" said Office Meyers.

"I mean I have a job for him if he wants it and even a place to stay."

"You mean above the clubhouse?" said Meyers.

"Yep. He could help Frank with the course maintenance and maybe even relieve me behind the bar once in awhile," Eileen said to the policeman before turning to face Lee. "You see, I own the *Crazy Horse Golf Club.* It's right outside Dying Tree. If you go straight on this road, you'll see the sign for it in another six and a half miles. I've been scrounging around for darn near two months for someone to help out at the golf course. Had ten applicants but not one of them seemed dependable and honest enough to hire. The job's yours but you're on probation the first thirty days. If things don't work out, I can terminate your employment with a week's notice."

"Working at a golf course? Are you kidding? It sounds wonderful! I accept," declared an ebullient Lee Wyatt.

"All right, load up your bike in the back and let's get going," began Eileen, "I bet Frank could use some help cutting the fairways on the back nine."

CHAPTER FIVE

He was halfway through cutting the grass of the fourteenth fairway. Frank had shown him how the John Deere riding lawn mower worked, watched him start it up, shift gears, and even go backwards. Satisfied his new assistant could handle the machine, Frank took off to work on the front nine. As Lee cruised through a vast open expanse of greenery, he admired the tracts of pines and birches following the rise of the Black Hills. On his right, a hundred yards away, Jackrabbit Creek (pronounced *crick* by the locals) meandered up the right side of the fairway. Twenty yards from the green, the creek leaned in and nipped its watery jaws at the edge of the putting surface. The holy smell of freshly mowed grass and country air surrounded him, filling up his soul with a lightness of spirit he couldn't recall ever feeling. Unlike before, he wasn't worried about what'd happen to him tomorrow or regretting something he'd done or failed to do yesterday. He was totally, completely immersed in the present moments of his life. Right now it was his sacred duty to cut the fairway of the fourteenth hole of Crazy Horse Golf Club.

On the ride through the town en route to the course, Lee noticed a queer change in the workings of his mind. Even though he knew his life back in Minnesota had been, in most respects, a giant lie, he couldn't help but try to recall the major parts of it, just because that was the way his mind normally worked. Like any person, it was natural to occasionally take the events and characters who'd filled part of their life and put them under the mind's microscope. When Lee tried to do that while sitting silently in the passenger's seat of Eileen Eide's Ford Bronco, he found it impossible to remember exactly what kind of job he had for all those years. He knew it was in an office but as to what he did for all those years and the names of his coworkers, those pieces of information squirmed away every time he was about to focus in on them. When he gave up trying to recall those things, he moved onto his home life. Besides knowing she was a woman and that her name had four letters, the particulars of his wife escaped him as well.

Then the most startlingly part of the episode happened. Instead of worrying whether he was losing his mind, Lee accepted the fact that he couldn't remember those things. Almost certainly he'd recall those details one day but if he didn't, he wouldn't worry about it. Like muck on the ocean floor, Lee let the sediments of his past settle quietly in the watery darkness.

He was now halfway through cutting the fourteenth fairway. A quick scan of the area revealed the thoroughness of his work. Lee handled the job, so far, flawlessly. Not a blade of glass had been missed. A broad smile raced across his face.

*   *   *

After finishing work at the golf course, Frank had asked him if he wanted to go to the shooting range with him. Lee told him he'd never shot a gun before, unless you counted a squirt gun and even that'd been thirty years ago. A smile escaped from beneath the deftly-constructed emotional wall Frank tended to keep in place around pretty much everyone.

"That's all right, Chief," he'd replied, "least if you start now, you'll be startin' late but you'll have one helluva teacher. Now normally I'm a modest, self-assuming kind a guy, but if I may be allowed a fanciful moment of immodesty, I'd say you couldn't find, at least around here, a better shot than yours truly. Besides the sheer joy of seein' a bullet tear through the exact spot you'd aimed for, shootin' helps me on the putting green. I find I'm more accurate, that my eyes are better after all that shootin'."

"You mean your physical eye or mind's eye?" Lee asked.

Frank fixed him with a steely-eyed glare that would have done Clint Eastwood proud.

"You can't separate the two, really, but I'd say it's mostly the mind's eye. If you got your act together upstairs, your body will follow. Anyway, you might as well come along. Hell, what else you got to do? You don't know Jack Shit here in Dying Tree—or Jill, for that matter. It's up to you. I normally go alone so don't feel obliged to come along just to humor me."

Lee shrugged his shoulders and said, "What the hell, why not? It could be fun."

And that's how Lee came to be at a shooting range with a man he'd met five hours ago. He watched as the old greens keeper and gunman fired off five straight bull's-eyes.

"Wow, you are good," Lee said, "I'd hate to be on your bad side."

"You just work hard and honest at the golf course and you'll forever be on my good side," he replied before blasting another bullet.

This one pierced the outer ring of the bull's-eye, the worst he'd had so far.

"Damn. Well, it's time for some new blood," he said while turning and handing the rifle to Lee.

Lee stared down the target, closing one eye while preparing to squeeze off a shot. He appeared ready to shoot but then suddenly glanced over at Frank.

"Do I need to cock it after each shot?"

Frank shook his head.

"It's a Browning Autoloader. It's got another seven shots left in it."

"All right."

He took aim, paused, and squeezed the trigger. Lee grunted after feeling the recoil. The bullet hit on the outermost ring of the target, nearly missing it altogether.

"Good Lord, get the women and children to a safe place," Frank laughed. "If the bull's-eye was the heart, you just put a bullet over the target's head. The only way you coulda hit any part of them was if that was Marge Simpson."

"You are quite the comedian, I must say," he replied. "Just don't forget who has the gun in his hands and despite my lack of accuracy, you're a helluva lot closer target than the bull's-eye."

Frank held up both arms in mock surrender.

"That's more like it. Let's show some respect for the apprentice gunslinger."

Lee turned and fired off another shot. This one was no better than the first. It was different, though. Instead of coming in high, it blasted a hole two feet below the target. This time Frank said nothing. He merely waited for his underling to fire again. The next shot was a few inches higher. The next shot after that was three inches higher. Three more shots brought increasingly more accurate results. The next shot missed the bull's-eye by two inches. Frank whistled.

"You're gettin' there, all right. You keep comin' here on a regular basis and there's no tellin' how damn good you'll get. And wait til you see what happens to your putting."

"That's what I'm curious about," he replied. "I hope you're right because I haven't broken 80 all year long. About four or five less putts a round is all I need to do it."

CHAPTER SIX

"In this scene, you're General Custer as a teen-age boy of fifteen or sixteen speaking with your father. He's just caught you peeking at your older sister changing clothes in her bedroom. This is a pivotal moment in the young man's life. The lesson he learns here will impact the rest of his heroic, though doomed life. He learns it's the group, whether it be family, neighborhood, community, state, and so on, that transcends individual desires or needs. Okay, are we clear on this?" asked Robert Meekins, director of "Massacre on the Prairie".

"Yeah, yeah, let's go," Ricky grumbled.

"All right, quiet on the set, everyone. Ricky, I want you over at the bedroom door peering in through the crack between the slightly open door and the door frame."

While Ricky strolled over to a door that appeared to open onto a real bedroom, Meekins yelled out, "Everyone quiet down! We're about to start rolling." A pause of five seconds, then, "Three, two, one . . . action."

The camera began rolling. On the set, all one saw was the young George Custer peeking through the crack in the slightly ajar door. They'd already filmed a scene with a 18-year-old blonde actress named Terry Baker undressing. Movie audiences would see alternating shots of George Custer as played by Ricky Mann (he wore a special facial mask made especially for the movie that made him look like a teenager and when he played the grown-up George Custer, he wore boots with lifts to make him look taller in addition to the genuine-appearing fake mustache and the rest of the make-up) and the other scene filmed separately of the disrobing young lady. Judicious, well-crafted editing would make it appear as though the young Custer was truly spying on his buxom older sister.

Lawrence Henry, a strapping, good-looking man in his early fifties with a mane of gray and black wavy hair, strode into the scene. The camera stayed on Ricky Mann even as Lawrence Henry's tobacco-edged, angry voice boomed out. The director wanted the audience to see the fear and surprise on the young man's face as his stern, intimidating father caught him up to no good. Ricky's head jerked toward the left where he saw the father stomping towards him.

"All right, god damned it, what the hell is goin' on here?"

"I didn't see a th-thing, Fa-father. Honest."

"Don't matter if you actually did or didn't. It's what you were tryin' to see. Important part is the intention."

"Whaddya me-mean, tension?"

"I mean. Oh shit, that's not the right," said Lawrence Henry, an expression of exasperation gripping his facial features. "It's not tension, it's *intention*, for Pete's sake. That's the third time you've screwed up this line."

"Hey, blown lines happen. It's part of the business. I thought after being an actor for all these years you'd know that by now. Of course, I suppose it's easier to memorize all your lines when all your roles are bit parts."

"For your information, I've had . . ."

Lawrence Henry, his tanned, weathered face almost turning another color, paused for three seconds. After blowing out a deep breath, the well-traveled actor said quietly but firmly, "Son, right off the top of my head, I could name five films I've been in that I've had roles far greater than bit parts. But I'm not going to waste my breath on a cocky little blowhard punk like you. I don't have to justify my acting career to anyone, but especially not to someone like you."

"Don't flatter yourself, old hoss," Ricky shot back. "Studios on tight budgets love to hire you because you work cheap. After MGM pays the top stars, they have to cut costs somewhere to help turn a buck."

"You have one skewed view of the world, little boy. One day you're going to run into a man or maybe even a group of men who aren't as civilized and nonviolent such as myself. But when you do, I dare say you're going to get your butt kicked," Lawrence said.

"Is that right—"

"All right, all right, that's enough. Let's call it quits for today. Come back tomorrow morning at six a.m. sharp. After several hours of blissful sleep, I'm sure we'll all feel much better," said Meekins.

"You won't see me back here tomorrow," declared Lawrence as he strode toward his dressing room to the left of the set. "Not with him in the movie. I only work with professionals. Real pros have class."

"Lawrence, please," said Meekins as he chased after the retreating six-footer. "I'm sure we can work out something here. You're perfect for the role of Custer's father. Let's go out somewhere for a bite to eat and maybe a drink. We need you in this picture . . ."

Ricky Mann shook his head as twin beams of contempt shot from his eyes and bored through Lawrence Henry's backside. He dismissed the veteran actor with a wave of the left hand before wheeling around and striding to his own dressing room that lay to the right of the set. Halfway there, his agent, Jim Morton, caught up with him. He looked comfortable enough in the forest-green cotton shorts and dark gray polo shirt. Blu-Blocker knock-offs dangled from a cord around his neck. Every time Morton took a step, the sunglasses slammed and bounced off his upper stomach. It seemed like the shades were attacking their owner in a desperate attempt to free themselves from the tie that enslaved them to their merciless owner.

"What's going on, Ricky? I thought you guys shot until around seven tonight."

"Bobby decided to cut it short," said Ricky. They were ten feet from his dressing room.

"Why's that?" Jim asked.

"Little disagreement on the set."

"Between who?"

Ricky ran an ATM-like card through the card reader. A red light lit up. He leaned a left shoulder into the door. It didn't budge.

"What the hell?" said Ricky.

"Flip the key card around," Jim offered. "The little white arrows should be facing down."

Ricky stared at him, his forehead scrunched up.

Jim grabbed the card and stuck it in the electronic-card reader, the white arrows pointed downwards like he'd told Ricky they should.

The door sprung open. Jim Morton followed his client into the capacious area. Ricky shut the door before locking it back up. It was really a misnomer to call what Ricky had here a dressing room. It wasn't a single room but several well furnished, fastidiously cleaned (by hired help) rooms. With a kitchen, living room, a bathroom featuring a claw-footed bathtub and Jacuzzi; study; and conference room complete with a twenty-foot long teakwood table and fully stocked wet bar; it was more like a penthouse apartment.

"You want anything to drink?" Ricky asked while heading toward the kitchen.

"No thanks," his agent replied. "So who was the disagreement between back on the set?"

"Bobby and the old fart," said Ricky as he returned with a bottle of Michelob. He twisted off the cap while dropping onto a leather couch standing in the middle of the living room. Jim found his normal spot at a small round table just to the left of the door.

"Bobby and Lawrence?" asked Jim with raised eyebrows. "That doesn't sound like Lawrence. He's an old pro. Been around the business for years. Doesn't bullshit around. He works hard, studies his lines, researches his role, does his job, and goes home. I can't imagine him—"

"It happened, all right!? Lawrence the fucking saint of an actor and Bobby had an argument. Bobby decided to let Lawrence cool off until tomorrow morning," Ricky lied, then followed it up with a gulp of beer.

"All right, all right, I believe you. But listen, we have to talk. Thomas Shearson called me today."

Ricky frowned while raising the Michelob to his lips.

"Thomas Shearson heads up the group of investors who were going to finance about thirty percent of the Ricky Mann Western Entertainment Complex right outside Dying Tree."

"Whaddya mean, 'were going to'?"

Jim stared down into the dangling sunglasses for several heartbeats before raising his head. His gaze met Ricky's.

"That's why he called me today. His group is pulling out of the deal."

"What!? They can't do that. We made a deal, goddamn it!! We'll sue the bastards. You call them up and tell them we'll slap a lawsuit on them so fast it'll—"

"That won't work. The agreement we signed contained a clause that gives them the right to back out if they couldn't arrange financing. Between the five of them, they'd raised about half of what we needed. They applied for a loan to obtain the rest but the bank turned them down."

"What if we kept them in but at half the original amount? Maybe we could find another group to take care of the other half they couldn't raise," Ricky said hopefully.

Jim shook his head.

"Nope. Shearson said it was an all or nothing deal. They wanted thirty percent or nothing. They're out of the picture," he said before parking the dark sunglasses on the ridge of his nose. He got up from the table and walked toward the kitchen. Halfway there, he turned back around. "You see, without them or someone to step in for them, the deal's dead."

"Fuck that. I'll throw in another ten percent. Then we only have to find someone to take care of the other twenty," said the movie star before pouring another fifth of the beer down his throat.

"Another possibility is not replacing the money Shearson would have put in and just scaling down the scope of the project. In that scenario, there'd be no golf course," said Jim.

"No, we have to have a golf course too. Dying Tree has plenty of casinos already, though of course this one will be bigger, better and more prestigious with my name associated with it, but even so, this has to be big enough to really make a splash. A casino alone won't do it. Besides, didn't you say something about golf courses being cash steers or gooses or some shit like that?"

The agent laughed.

"I said once the course is built and marketed properly and with any kind of management, it becomes a cash cow. Or you could say it's the goose that lays the golden egg. But you do have a point there. If the deal is done, we need to have both a casino and golf course. That said, now we have to find another investor group as soon as possible. I'll go through my Rolodex and e-mail address book and generate a hit list. Hopefully we can get a few nibbles before the week is done."

"Okay. Keep me posted," Ricky said while studying the label on the beer bottle.

"I will. I'll send you an e-mail tonight or tomorrow if there's any developments. Now Ricky, there is one more thing we should discuss. This may be nothing, you know, just a bullshit rumor reported by rags that print that kind of garbage because there's a big market for that kind of stuff, but I've heard—"

"That I'm doing methamphetamines. Yeah, yeah, I read the fucking article in Star Watch. Like you said, it's bullshit. I guess they were short of space that week and had to make up something. Naturally the first thing I thought of was suing the hell out of them but lawsuits take forever to settle and half the time or more you don't win 'em anyway."

"Plus it's a major distraction that requires so much mental and emotional energy that it can detract from your acting ability. I don't have to tell you that roles require an actor's complete commitment. If you're thinking about something else while on the set, your performance can't possibly be as good as it should be," said Jim.

"Damn right," Ricky said. He stretched out on the sofa, crossing his legs at the ankles. The actor watched his agent, financial advisor and long-time friend head for the door. Three feet from it, Jim Morton stopped dead, wheeled and faced Ricky.

"Of course, if someday by some strange chance you actually did start doing methamphetamines or a similar substance, that itself would hinder your acting abilities far more than any lawsuit. More importantly, repeated use would threaten your health, both spiritual and physical."

"Hey, I said I'm not doing any of that shit. All I need I got right here," he said while grabbing the Michelob.

"I know, I know, but I'm just playing the role of a surrogate father for a minute or two. Humor me, okay? You won't get the full lecture but as a friend and an experienced entertainment guy who's been around the Hollywood scene for sixteen years, I'm just giving some words of caution. I don't care who offers you any. Doesn't matter if it's a starlet, rich babe or call girl. Don't experiment with any of these street drugs, especially stimulants like speed or coke, because all it takes is one good high to hook you. I've seen it happen to people. After they're hooked, you can tell. Whenever you're talking to them, it's like they're not really, truly there talking to you. Their body is there but in their mind, they're thinking about their next high. Or if they've already taken the drug, you can certainly tell. All that phony, fake, trumped-up energy. It's easy to tell either way. At least for me it is."

"Thanks for the pep talk but I'm fine," declared Ricky. "Like I said, beer is as much as I ever need to alter my state of mind."

Jim said nothing for five seconds, then said, "Good. Don't change that part of yourself. I'd hate to see you dragged down into the muck like the others."

Two more steps brought him to the door. He turned the handle, pulled the door open, and said, "Take care, buddy. I'll get back to you on the Dying Tree deal as soon as I hear anything."

"Sounds good."

"Bye."

Jim Morton disappeared behind the closed door. Suddenly Ricky felt cold. He hopped up and went directly to the thermometer. He turned it up to 78 degrees, five degrees higher than its previous setting. Thirty minutes later, while sitting at the kitchen table contemplating a bowl of Campbell's tomato soup, he still felt chilled to his core. Something about the visit with Jim left him frightened and cold. Ricky shoveled in the last of the soup before sticking the bowl and spoon in the dishwasher. He grabbed another Michelob from the fridge before returning to the kitchen table. Ricky twisted the cap off the top of the bottle, executed a series of fakes, whirled and launched the bottle cap toward the plastic wastebasket wedged in the far corner of the room. It struck the wall, bounced diagonally until striking the kitchen cabinet hugging the right side of the wastebasket and then disappeared into the container's depths.

"I can't believe it, sports fans, Ricky Mann does it again! What an incredible shot. Over three seven-foot defenders, with time running out, the Laker guard makes the shot that gives them a stunning victory. Lakers win, Lakers win, Lakers win . . ."

He had done speed and coke. However, he'd never done methamphetamines—yet. Before his old friend and agent had showed up today, the star had told himself that the next time someone at one of the cast parties (or any party, for that matter) offered him methamphetamines or a similar substance, he wouldn't refuse it like he'd done in the past. The allure of the otherworldly experience, like an impatient child at their father's pant leg, tugged hard and long on his soul. He knew he should shun any kind of drug-induced high but all his life he'd been a rebel. Going against the grain was natural for him. He'd come to expect himself to sit on the opposite side of the couch from the rest of society. Conformity and Ricky Mann simply were not compatible. Taking drugs when the rest of society said he shouldn't was something he envisioned himself doing quite easily.

He hadn't felt the urge to be rebellious since moving out to Hollywood eight years ago. At first just being in show business and making all that money had been enough excitement. Sure, he'd went out to bars and attended parties and such but he'd only been offered drugs ten, maybe twelve times, during all his years out here. Up until recently, the right choice had been clear. Rejecting the offers had become easy but lately they'd grown more enticing. A void had crept into the house of his heart. To fill that empty spot, he required a special substance, something that could transport him to a special place. The high of fame and money had been enough for awhile.

Of course, the money in itself was nothing. It's what you did with the money. Wealth was like an extremely productive locksmith. It'd opened so many doors for Ricky. Behind those doors were all manner of life: a mansion so big and brimming with Byzantine passageways that first-time visitors needed a map or blind luck to find their back out; rounds of golf with rich men and women at courses perched along oceans or on mountain tops; parties in San Francisco and New York City with tables of food that seemed to stretch on as far as the oceans poised alongside the respective cities; letters and phone calls from mayors, governors, senators and Congressmen from all over the United States and even from a few foreign leaders; unbridled adoration from autograph-seeking fans at various public appearances.

Those things had satisfied his hunger for excitement and adventure for a long time. Now he'd reached the point where his inner dialogue was basically, BEEN THERE, DONE THAT. He'd traveled as much he cared to in a physical, spatial sense. What he sought now was a journeying to a different state of mind. After all, wasn't that the ultimate quest? The inner realm, though impossibly expansive, was rarely explored beyond the safe, known territory. Like the old Wild West heroes whom Ricky frequently portrayed, he had a wanderlust that kept him from ever being too satisfied staying in one place for very long. One form of travel was moving along the different levels of consciousness. Beyond drunkenness and the recent coke—and speed-induced highs, he was an admittedly inexperienced traveler of the states of mind. He very much wanted to change that. The exploration was there for the taking. All that was required was courage, a source of substances to take one to the promised states and sufficient funds to purchase the required drugs. He had the first and last, thereby leaving him to only find the middle one. With all his party-circuit friends, solving that problem would be a piece of cake.

Ricky swigged more beer, then got up to fetch a sweater from the upstairs bedroom.

CHAPTER SEVEN

"What'd you do back in, where was it you said you're from?" asked Frank Leeds.

"It's not important," responded Lee as he checked out the traffic around them. They were about halfway between the golf course and downtown Dying Tree.

"You tryin' to hide something?" asked Frank. He turned a tight left perhaps three seconds before a semi blasted through the intersection.

"No, not at all. I just think my old life is only that—my old life. What I am now should be the result of my thoughts and actions in my new life. The more I invoke my past, the more enslaved I am to it. Does that make any sense?"

Frank rustled up a Marlboro 100, lit it and took a deep drag. After peering into the cloud of carcinogenic vapor, he said, "In some metaphysical, psychological, mumbo-jumbo way, yes. But since I think all that stuff is overrated, I think you're fulla shit. Nothing personal, ah course. So far you've been a great worker and you seem like a nice, honest guy. If you're a little wacko about some things, I say it's no big deal as long as you don't hurt anyone else. You're not prone to sudden fits of violence, are you?"

"Just on the golf course after a shooting a triple," he quipped.

"I've been known to cuss and break an occasional club after holes like those so I got no problem with that."

Frank turned right into a public parking lot. A pimply, skinny high school boy told them the place would be full before too long. Frank gave the kid a five, who then pointed out the nearest open spot. After easing into a space between a new black Jimmy and a jazzy, ready-to-race, red Mazda, he shut off the engine.

"What are you in the mood for?" asked Frank.

Lee threw him a blank look. He shrugged, then managed, "I don't know. Anywhere that serves beer and is reasonably quiet. If they serve decent food, that'd be a bonus but I'm not that hungry just yet. Oh yeah, and someplace with pool tables."

As they left the truck, Frank said, "I know just the place."

The two breezed through the darkening night air, Lee letting Frank lead the way. Up Main Street they trod, past middle-aged and older gamblers who lugged large plastic cups filled with quarters, dimes and nickels. Two chartered buses rolled past them, the tinted windows leaving the passengers looking like someone had mixed together all the colors at their disposal. An employee of an establishment hollowly announced the dinner special for tonight—"Baby back ribs and all the fixin's for only $5.95, immediate seating available"—but Lee was more interested in drink than food. Frank seemed to think along similar lines. They pressed on.

Two blocks later, Frank stopped and turned to Lee. He jerked a thumb over his shoulder.

"This is it. Whaddya think?"

Lee looked up at the sign: CLEAR SKY SALOON.

"What's so special about this place?"

"The bar got its name from the fact that many a well-known actor and actress have been spotted in the place because of the identity of the establishment's owner."

"Oh so one can see, like looking into a clear night sky, many stars?" Lee asked.

"That's right," answered Frank. "None other than Ricky Mann owns the place."

"Won't it be crowded? I mean with him being a celebrity and all—"

Frank snorted.

"Nah. I mean it used to be crowded as hell right after Ricky's first coupla movies but now it's not too bad. There's actually three levels. The first level is a small casino and bar. The second floor is the fancy-smancy restaurant, you know, waiters with white towels on their arms and customers putting cloth napkins in their laps, that kinda shit. The third level is a dark little bar and grill with three pool tables stuck in a rear corner. I'm not crazy about all the Ricky Mann shit stuck all over but it's damn near impossible to find decent pool tables in this town."

"Sounds good to me. Let's do it," Lee said.

They ducked inside.

"This way," Frank whispered, taking a hard left at the hostess stand which was twenty feet from the front entrance. Lee, after checking out a life-size statue of the business' owner, followed his friend. They breezed down an almost empty hallway. Frank angled right with Lee right behind. A gold-plated elevator shone in the dimness at the end of the hall. After little more than a minute of waiting, the door split open. Eight people filed out, two of them apparently more inebriated than the rest as they laughed and spoke in entirely excessive volumes. Lee and Frank slipped into the car. The car zipped them up to the third floor.

After exiting the elevator, Frank led the way down a hallway lined with photographs, paintings, and advertisements from Ricky Mann's movies. Ricky as a gunslinger known as Stu "One-Eye" Grimson in *Frontier Showdown*, then Ricky in *Journey Into The Endless Night*, a rare departure into the horror genre, and then the young star as Robby "Dead On" Dale in *Dakota Uprising*. Rounding out the tunnel of tribute were photos from two gangster flicks, one Vietnam war epic, and finally, at the very end of the hallway, an ad for *Horse Droppings*, a western parody in which Ricky portrayed Dynamite Darcy Smith, a bisexual sheriff who preferred studying Shakespeare and Milton to running in outlaws. By the time they reached an empty table, Lee wasn't sure if he loved or loathed the guy.

After rounding the corner, Lee found they weren't entirely free from the Ricky Mann parade of movies. Though more widely disbursed, the native son's mug in its various guises was much in evidence. Peering down from the ceiling, hanging on the walls by tables, and looking up from souvenir plastic cups in a display case by the cash register, it was too obvious to be subliminal. Certainly this was nothing like flashing an image of a Coke on a movie screen so quickly moviegoers didn't even realize it'd happened. This was more like hiring someone to walk up and down the aisles with a sandwich board with Coca Cola splashed all over it. Still, it was better than the hallway. At least in here there were scattered places of refuge from the assault.

"What's your poison?" Frank asked.

"Bud," he said, then quickly said, "No, strike that. Is there any local or regional beer that's really good?"

"Hell, I don't know. I guess the best known one is one from a brewery 'bout five miles from here. It's called Pete and Dave's Sizzling Pepper Brew—SPB for short. Every bottle has a hot chili pepper at the bottom. Too damn spicy for my tastes but there's a goodly number of folks who drink the stuff, I guess."

"All right, you sold me, partner. I'll take one of those bad boys, please."

Frank grunted something before striding toward the bar. Having set the intoxicating beverage procurement process firmly in motion, Lee struck out for the right-hand rear part of the bar. Three pool tables hunched together as if seeking body warmth to help them against the arctic climate created by the air-conditioning. Lee wished he'd brought a sweater but the thought never crossed his mind until now. It was summertime, after all. He briefly considered asking one of the bartenders to turn it down but shrugged off the idea. Like winters in the Midwest, he'd just have to get used to it.

Lee tried out four pool cues before discovering one that was heavy enough and mostly free from warping. Frank reappeared, the beers in hand.

"Find a suitable weapon, Wild Bill?" he joked while setting the bottles on a round table five feet from the pool table.

"Matter a fact I did, Pilgrim. Now git your own weapon and I'll show you how to shoot," said Lee in his best John Wayne voice. Frank shot him an expression that told Lee the impression wasn't even good enough to merit a verbal response. While his opponent chose a cue, he stuck four quarters in the slots and proceeded to rack the balls. By the time he was done racking, Frank was ready to do some breaking.

"Step aside, city boy. With the power of this break, I can't guarantee all the balls'll stay on the table," warned Frank as he bent over to line up the shot.

"Yeah, yeah, talk is cheap," Lee replied while ambling away from the table.

A crack like the snapping of a bone pierced the air. The cue ball, after blasting into the triangle of balls, hopped nine inches into the air, landed and spun crazily back away from the melee. The variously colored balls scattered like soldiers after a grenade had been tossed in their midst. The four and six balls dropped into pockets while three stripes came to rest right by pockets.

"Lucky break," said Lee after he'd climbed onto a barstool.

Frank grunted as if barely hearing him, which was probably the case. He studied the green felt landscape for several seconds, nodded to himself, and bent down to line up for a shot on the one ball. Just like at the firing range, Frank's aim was true. The ball disappeared down the hole like Alice's rabbit friend in Wonderland. His opponent proceeded to pocket three more balls. However, after sinking the last shot, a nifty side pocket bank on the seven, Frank found the cue ball separated from his last two balls by a wall of stripes. At first Lee assumed Frank'd have to try banking the cue ball off the side rail. His friend surprised by jumping the white ball over the striped ones. Luckily for Lee, the three ball didn't go in.

"Well I'll be dipped in liquid fertilizer," Lee drawled.

"Son, that can be arranged," shot back Frank.

"Maybe another day. I can only have so much fun during any 24-hour period. Otherwise I go stark raving mad. Well, now that you've got most of your damn balls out of the way, this should be easy."

Frank snorted. Lee went to work on the table. By the time the chalk from his pool cue settled, five stripes had joined the five solids in the pockets. His opponent had drained all his beer by the time he got up to shoot.

"Not bad for a rookie," Frank said while approaching the table. He turned his gaze to the layout of the five remaining balls. The eight ball had ended up only a few inches from where it began the game while Frank's two solids—the three and five—laid four inches apart up against the rail behind where the eight ball rested. Lee's thirteen and fifteen balls were in the middle of table, not more than eighteen inches from the eight. The thirteen effectively blocked any possible shot on the five. Frank's only shot, it seemed, was either a cut or bank on the three ball. While Frank considered his options, two men, both wearing cowboy hats and boozy smiles, strode toward the pool tables. The taller one had snuff tucked his left cheek while his buddy chomped on a cigar. Both had their hands around full bottles of Grain Belt. Frank flicked a quick visual scan at the sound of their approach before resuming his thoughtful posture. While the two cowboys rifled through the rack in search of cue sticks, Frank decided on his strategy.

"Three back in this corner," he announced while nodding at the pocket he meant.

Lee snuck in a sip of beer while watching the three carom off the rail and roll along toward the intended pocket.

"Nice shot, Frank," Lee said as the ball neared the pocket.

"Ain't in yet," he replied.

Sure enough, though close, the shot didn't fall. The red three struck the tip of the pocket and bounced away.

"Damn, helluva try. I thought you had it."

"Nah, I knew it wasn't in the second I hit. Tell you what, I'm gonna grab another cold one. You want another one?"

Lee saw there was only a few drops left in his bottle.

"Sure. I'll wait 'til you get back before I shoot."

Frank nodded and angled for the rectangular bar area. Lee settled in to watch the two new arrivals on the adjacent table. The taller one yanked out a twenty-dollar bill and tossed it on the side rail.

"Whaddya say, Petey old boy, you wanna go twenty bucks on this one?"

His friend hesitated, then dug into his back pocket for his wallet. After examining the contents, he said, "Okay, you're on," and proceeded to throw a ten and two fives on top of the twenty.

"Lag for break?" said the taller one. Pete, the cigar-wielder, nodded.

The taller one went first. He hit it too hard, the cue ball coming to rest a full foot from the rail. Pete nailed his shot just two inches away.

"That's probably the best damn shot you'll have all night," said the taller one before swigging from the bottle of Grain Belt.

"First of many, Eddie. You'll see."

Pete laid the cigar in an ash tray on the round table in back of the pool table and then got the cue ball where he wanted it. Lee watched the white ball blast off the one. The rest of the balls scattered in every direction. Only the four ball dropped but the rest of the solids and most of the stripes were spread out nicely. It looked like Pete could make a bunch of balls if he played it right but if he didn't, Eddie would have several options. Either way, Lee thought this'd be a pretty short game.

There were four customers ahead of Frank at the bar. It'd be a few minutes before Frank returned so Lee relaxed and resumed watching the other game. Pete was a pretty good shot, though the first five that went in were relatively easy because of the object balls' nearness to the pockets. The break had been so good that it meant the shooter didn't have to be as good with the other shots. Still, he seemed confident enough, the stroke of the cue unhesitating, the follow-through complete on each shot. The taller one, Eddie, had grown steadily quieter throughout the display. After Pete sunk a long cut shot on the one ball, Eddie rolled his eyes and downed the rest of his beer. Lee cast a look toward the bar. Frank had moved up to the second spot in line. His progress was slow but steady.

Returning to the other game, Lee saw Pete knock the seven ball in a corner pocket. The cue rolled to a stop in the middle of the table. Despite the presence of all the stripes, he had a clear shot at the eight ball.

"You little fuck head, what the hell got into you? You never play this good," said Eddie.

"Oh you're just pissed off 'cause you're gonna lose a twenty spot," Pete replied.

"No, I'm serious, goddamned it. I can't remember the last time you ran the table. In fact, I betcha you've never run a table in your life," said Eddie derisively, then walked over to his opponent's cigar. He snatched up the stogie.

"You know, smokin's bad for you. Tell you what, I'm gonna do you a favor," said Eddie right before he doused the cigar in Pete's bottle of beer. Ashes dropped and floated lazily in the container.

"You cock sucking son of a whore!" yelled Pete after straightening up. "What the hell's wrong with you? You that broke that twenty bucks means that much to you? Well I guess I'd probably be concerned about twenty dollars if I'd been without a job as long as you have," said Pete before bending over to line up what could be the last shot of the game.

Lee shot a glance at the bar. The bartender was handing two beers to Frank. Returning to the unfolding drama on the other table, he saw Pete bring the cue back. Right before the forward stroke, Eddie hollered, "Don't miss."

Pete missed. The eight ball rattled off both tips of the side pocket and stopped rolled to a stop six inches from the intended target. The shooter straightened up immediately and stalked toward his opponent.

"You piece of shit. That's it, you forfeit the game," Pete declared while leaning to grab the money from the side rail. Eddie was too fast, however, the taller one snapping up the bills just before he could. Eddie danced over to the other side of the table, waving the money in the air.

"'Fraid not, partner. In fact, as a penalty for your abusive language, you forfeit the game and the money."

"Put the money back down. Let's just finish the game. I've decided to forgive you for the cheap little stunt you pulled right when I was shooting. I mean you're so far behind anyway that there's so little chance of you winning the game. But hey, I'll give you a chance."

"Are you kidding? I've beaten better players than you after bein' this far behind. Don't fuckin' flatter yourself," said Eddie as he slowly laid the money back down on the side rail in front of him.

"You're such a dickhead. Why can't you admit you're not that good of a player, especially considering how damn much you play," said Pete.

Eddie dropped his cue stick and stormed around the pool table to where his opponent stood. Pete froze for a heartbeat, then quickly leaned his cue against the wall behind him. Eddie had his fists up, his eyes ablaze and cheeks inflamed with anger. Pete braced himself for a fight, his own fists up.

"We'll see who the dickhead is," said Eddie as he took two more steps. Before Lee even realized it, he'd lept up from the barstool. His feet were carrying him into the middle of the impending altercation.

"Hold on there," he heard himself shout, "you two don't really want to do this."

Both their faces turned toward Lee. While Eddie scowled, Pete cast a bewildered look at the approaching stranger.

"Who the fuck are you?" Eddie demanded.

"It's not important. What's important is that you should really stand back and think about what you're about to do. I mean, it sounds like you two are good friends. Why do something you're both going to regret tomorrow and for a long time after that? You should be able to settle this without beating each other's brains out, right?"

Eddie was about to say something but no words came out. Pete nodded and said, "Well, yeah, I hope so. Eddie's not really a dickhead. I don't know why I said that but most of the time, he's really a good guy."

"Well, ah, thanks. I, I . . . I guess I said a coupla things I shouldn't have either. Let's just finish the damn game, okay?"

"Deal," replied Pete. He turned to Lee.

"Thanks. Say, what's your name anyway?"

Lee waved the question away while turning around to begin the short trip back to his barstool by their pool table.

"Doesn't matter. Go on now. Finish the game."

Eddie shrugged, then said to Pete, "Your shot, buddy."

By now, Frank had set the beers on the round table. He smiled at Lee.

"Holy shit, I go to get a coupla beers and all hell almost breaks loose. Good job on keepin' the peace, Tex. Guess we got a new sheriff in town."

"Yeah right. Okay, can I shoot now?"

"Go right ahead."

Lee grasped his stick and went to work.

CHAPTER EIGHT

Lee sat behind an oak desk, his leather cowboy boots set firmly on the wooden floor. Across the room, sitting on the edge of a metal cot behind iron bars, sat Lindy "Sidewinder" Smith. Lee'd thrown his outlaw ass in jail last night after Lindy had raced up and down Main Street firing his six-guns straight up in the air. Though no one was hurt, Lindy broke the town ordinance that prohibited the carrying of firearms in downtown Dodge City. If the Lee didn't make an example of old Sidewinder Smith, the town's swelling outlaw element might very well take over the settlement. There'd be random shooting in Dodge's streets, upstanding citizens in the line of fire. As the new sheriff, Lee Wyatt Earp simply would not abide that.

The new sheriff was diligently filling out an arrest report when suddenly the door to the jailhouse burst open. It was Bill Cody, one of three deputies under the sheriff's chain of command.

"Sheriff, sheriff, you gotta come outside quick," Bill said in a breathless tone.

"What is it, Billy?" Lee responded, the baritone voice tinged with a drawl.

"Texas Tommy and his gang just rode into town. They tied up their horses and went into Al's Saloon. Tommy's been braggin' about how they're gonna spring our prisoner. Said no member of their gang is gonna be locked for very long."

Sheriff Lee slowly stood up. After hitching up his pants and running his hands over the two Colt 45's holstered on either side of him, he drawled, "They're gonna hafta shoot me dead first."

"I think that's pretty much what they're fixin' on doin'," said the deputy.

From inside the cell, Sidewinder Smith laughed like a donkey. He leaned forward, his crooked nose protruding through the bars while both hands gripped the bars.

"Hell Sheriff, you haven't a got a chance. There's at least six a them, maybe seven or eight. Unless you can round up your other deputies in an awful big hurry, it's gonna be just you and your deputy here against Texas Tommy's gang."

"Don't be includin' me in that number," the deputy began, "I got a wife and four kids to think of. I'm gettin' outta here. Sorry Sheriff."

"Don't you worry, son. If we all follow our hearts, all will be for the best," he began while striding toward the door leading outside. "You got a family of four, five includin' yerself, to protect. I got me a whole town to think of."

"Sheriff Lee, this town ain't never seen the likes of you. In fact, I don't expect Dodge'll ever have a lawman as brave and pure as you," gushed the deputy.

"Aw shucks, Bill, there you go again. Makin' me blush and all . . ."

Lee sat straight up in bed. He shook his head. That was the last straw. The last line was simply too much to handle. But now that he'd woken up, he felt better with each second he put between himself and the dream. He chuckled. Talk about bad western movies. His dream was as bad as any he'd ever seen. So bad it was funny.

"Must be this South Dakota air," he said while laying his head back on the pillow. He flipped from his left side onto his right one. "Or maybe it was those three chili pepper beers. Damn, I won't be doing that again."

Convinced the worst dreams were behind him, Lee shifted into power-snoozing mode. Ten minutes later, the gears finally meshed. The confused, superficial, contradictory messages of conventional reality were forsaken for the purer realm of conscious-less sleep.

*   *   *

He'd just seen this hole three hours ago. Back then he was trimming the fringe and raking the bunkers. After Eileen told him and Frank to knock off early, instead of leaving the course, they played it. Though he had intentionally not kept track of his total score through six holes (he felt less pressure that way), he would figure it out after the round was over. However, he knew he was taking far fewer putts than he usually did. By god, Frank might be right about target shooting helping his putting.

On this hole, a four-hundred-twenty-yard par-four with a pond lurking to the left of the green, Lee got on in three. He was happy to have successfully avoided the watery killer of good golf scores to the green's left. Still, his ball sat on the front right part of the putting surface. The hole was fifty feet and one tier away. The incline separating this level from the upper one sloped harshly to the right but the terrain around the hole sloped back to the left. Frank's chip left him fifteen feet below the hole. He'd marked his ball.

"Breaks more to the left than most people think," said Frank.

"Is that right?" Lee replied.

Frank nodded.

"Thanks. I'll keep that in mind."

He stood behind the ball, gauged the distance to the hole, considered how much more the slope to the left was than the right, and lined up accordingly. One practice stroke and then he hit the putt. The white sphere rolled up the onto the upper tier, well right of the hole as Lee'd planned. Then it began curving back to the left. For a perhaps two seconds, Lee thought he'd hit the putt too soft. His fear was needless, however, as the Top Flite hit the downward slope twelve feet from the hole. Now the ball was moving downhill and breaking left at the same time. Frank craned his neck to get a better look. Lee almost looked away.

"Looks good," Frank remarked when the ball was five feet from the target.

Though the putt was still moving from right to left, it was no longer traveling downhill. That meant the speed had lessened as well. Again Lee wondered if he'd hit the putt with enough authority to get the ball to the hole.

Three feet away.

Two feet.

One.

The ball grazed the left side of the cup, caught the rim, followed the edge of the hole like a basketball that rolls around the rim, and then spun out. It stopped two inches from the cup.

"Damn it!" Lee exclaimed. "Did you see that? I was robbed."

"That was a helluva putt, partner. But I wouldn't get too agitated. A two-putt from where you were at is no small feat. That goes to show how far you've come in a short time with your short game."

Lee thought about it. He was right.

"Yeah. I'll gladly take that," he said. Lee walked up and tapped the putt in for a five.

CHAPTER NINE

The white Mercedes, windows tinted to conceal the faces inside, rolled into Dying Tree just before six o'clock on this Friday afternoon. For the citizens of the town, the tinted windows meant little. They knew who was inside by the customized license plate.

RICKYM. The native-son-turned-movie-star, Ricky Mann, had come back for a visit. At least ten people walking along Main Street waved at the passing car, though they knew they probably wouldn't ever know if the object of their admiration returned their wave. No matter. He'd put Dying Tree on the map and that was enough.

The spotless Mercedes eased to a stop in front of the Clear Sky Saloon. Two young men and their female companions, neither of them more than eighteen, waited breathlessly for the doors to open so their hero might emerge into the sunlight and wind, proving he was human just like the rest of them. Eventually that possibility became reality. Ricky arose, his rugged, tanned face appearing with the trademark Blublockers perched over a crooked but famous nose. Wearing tight designer blue jeans, black polo shirt and snakeskin cowboy boots, Ricky, flanked by two meaty, pissed-off-looking security guards, strolled into the front entrance of the Clear Sky Saloon. The crowd around the car had grown from four to at least twenty-five. Two teenage girls squealed with delight and one young male expressed a serious desire to obtain the star's autograph. Both were unceremoniously ignored as the entourage—Ricky's agent, personal trainer, two attractive women—one raven-haired, the other strawberry blonde and both almost busting right out of their tee-shirts, and two more security guards—rounded out the group.

Once through the main entrance, Ricky flashed a smile upon seeing the life-size statue of himself standing tall on a three-foot high pedestal next to the hostess station. After admiring his likeness, the movie star moved on.

He'd called Al Mann, his brother, from the cell phone while riding into town from the airport. They agreed to meet in the restaurant for dinner and a few drinks. Within five minutes, they were sitting down in the private dining room in the very back of the restaurant. Ricky rarely ate in the regular dining area because of excess attention from the customers. Everyone wanted a piece of him, it seemed.

"The usual, Ricky?" asked Doug Stanton, the manager of the restaurant now helping out behind the bar. The usual for the actor was a Smirnoff's Vodka martini with two olives.

"Yeah but make it real, real dry. In fact, just wave the vermouth bottle over the glass," quipped Ricky as he leaned on the counter while Doug poured the drink.

"What about your food order?" asked Doug as he dropped two olives on top the glass of ice and vodka.

"Just a chef's salad. This meal is gonna be heavy on liquid, light on the food," Ricky said with a dark twinkle in his eye. Doug handed him the drink.

"Put it on your tab?" he joked.

"You got it, pardner." Ricky replied with an exaggerated drawl reminiscent of his role in *Horse Droppings*, the western parody from six years ago. Ricky leaned over so his face hung above the bar counter. He motioned for Doug to come closer. Nearby Tom Motley, part-time bartender, took a drink order from a cocktail waitress. After Doug was close enough, the actor said quietly, "You see those two young ladies over there, the two who came in with me?"

"Sure. Hard to miss something like that," he replied. "Why?"

"They're friends of mine, sort of business acquaintances, you might say, from out on the coast. They're between acting jobs right at the moment. I told them they could earn a few dollars this weekend. I was thinkin' they could help serve drinks in the main dining room. They could take the six to two shift tonight and tomorrow."

Doug frowned.

"I don't know. I mean, we're pretty well set for drink servers. Norma and Francine are on both nights—"

"Tell you what, here's what you do. Give Norma tonight off and Francine tomorrow. With pay, of course. Tell 'em it's a reward for their many years of service."

"They're not gonna like that. I most of what they make isn't the wage we pay 'em. It's the tips they get . . ."

"Listen, I don't give a horse's ass if they like it or not. It's only one night and it's a management decision they're gonna have to live with. If it upsets those gals too much, there's about forty or fifty other places in town they can go work at."

Doug sighed, rolled his eyes and looked for something to do. He spotted a couple of dirty glasses that could use washing.

"Yeah, you're right about that, all right. Plenty of places in Dying Tree for bar maids and such to find work. But I'll tell you what, it's been my experience that the best businesses are the ones that treat the employees like long-time, good friends. You treat them with respect and care about what happens to them. You do that, and you earn their trust and loyalty. Of course, the bottom line is always looking at what's best for the business. You put your best, most capable people in the most challenging positions so that your customers are best served. Like serving drinks on the busiest shifts. You don't need rocket scientists but damn it, you need servers who're familiar with different kinds of drinks, are alert enough to know where all their customers are and know how long it's been since they last ordered a drink, and so on. With all the noise in here and the staff runnin' around, if you get someone new to the job who's easily rattled, you got real problems."

"Listen, I own this place. I don't need no damned business school lecture. I'm fucking tellin' you the way it's gonna be. Understood?" said Ricky, his eyes narrowed so much that from a distance, it'd appear he was sleeping.

Doug Stanton said nothing, He started cleaning one of the marginally dirty glasses he spotted. Halfway through, the slender-framed, clean-cut manager turned back around to face Ricky. He flashed a look at the two "actresses" standing fifteen feet away. They were listening to a local drunk ramble on about the weather and how their flight from Hollywood was or some such shit.

"Yeah, I understand. In fact, I'm beginning to understand you real good."

"Good. Then I'll tell Anne and Nikki the goods news," Ricky said while stepping away from the bar. He hadn't gone five feet when he heard Doug Stanton's voice.

"Say Ricky, there's one more thing you should know about the game of Life."

Ricky stopped, then slowly pivoted toward Doug.

"And what might that be?"

By now Doug was onto the second dirty glass.

"If you treat people like shit long enough, the sewer's gonna back up on you."

Ricky laughed and turned around to tell Anne and Nikki of their new temporary positions.

*   *   *

Fifteen minutes later, Al arrived. By then, Ricky was on his second martini. Al ordered a Grain Belt while he mulled over what to order for dinner. When the server returned with his beer, Al ordered the beef ribs dinner. After each man sipped their respective beverages, Al cleared his throat as he looked up from his beer.

"I understand you're thinkin' 'bout building a casino and golf course on the north edge of town."

"That's right."

"How's it lookin'?" Al asked.

"Pretty damn good. Why?" Ricky said.

Al grasped the amber bottle, peered at the Grain Belt label, then looked up at his younger brother.

"Oh, I don't know. After talkin' with a few people who know about business and finances and such, I hear they're real concerned about the deal. They're sayin' it if the deal falls through, the city stands to lose a whole lot of money. Maybe lose enough to declare bankruptcy."

"Who in the hell told you that bullshit?" demanded Ricky.

"Tom Burnett, who's a CPA in town, and Bob Keller, who's the principal shareholder in the First Union Bank and Trust down on Old Main Street," said his brother.

Ricky smiled and shook his head. He sipped his drink, then said, "Well they're fulla fuckin' shit, I'd say. This city has a damned gold mine here with all the profitable businesses, most of them casinos, bars, restaurants, or some combination. The sales and property tax rate is higher than almost any city or town in the whole damn state."

"That is true but in the last three years, they have been hit hard with expenses. The last two winters had record snowfall, which means they had to pay the snowplow drivers all that overtime plus buyin' new equipment 'cause the old stuff was really old. Then the flood from last year wiped out sixty percent of the homes and thirty percent of the businesses. Even though a lotta individuals and businesses got federal disaster relief, there were some who didn't. The city agreed to help them out financially. And of course we got the construction of the new city hall and sports arena comin' in at three and half million dollars. The city's got serious debt problems. And with the state of South Dakota havin' to bail out all those farmers, there just isn't any extra government money to send to little old Dying Tree. We're pretty much on our own. Any business deals the city makes in the near future future has got to produce positive results. Otherwise, well, the town's in deep shit."

"Don't you worry, little brother, old Ricky will come through. I mean, think about it for a minute. The city of Dying Tree is investing in an enterprise with my name associated with it. Just imagine it: a casino and golf course owned by Ricky Mann and a few other minor owners. I mean come on, a hometown boy who's a national, damn, make that international star. Think of how many people are going to go there just because of the name. Once they go there and see how pretty it is and the great customer service and layout of the golf course, they'll keep comin' back. This, little brother, is gonna be so damn BIG you can't even imagine it."

Ricky tilted his wooden, straight-back chair onto two legs, blew out a breath, and said, "But of course it's hard for some folks around here to grasp this. I mean, it takes some imagination and vision to see what I'm talkin' about. People who can't see beyond own narrow little lives will be against it, I'm sure."

"Vision and imagination can be a wonderful thing," began Al, "but they have to be backed up with a realistic plan for success. If you have that, then things will be fine."

"Everything is gonna work out. I guarantee it," Ricky stated.

"That's good to hear, brother, it really is. If you're right, the whole town will be happy. If not . . ."

Al allowed that unpleasant possibility to circulate high over them.

"But if you're wrong—"

Ricky's hand shot up like a switchblade.

"I said everything is gonna be fine," he said, his voice tinged with irritation.

"I sure hope so," Al said. After a sip from his beer, he said, "Enough of this business talk. You wanna come over to the house tomorrow night for supper? Debbie says you'd probably appreciate a good home-cooked meal. I'm not sure exactly what she's plannin' on makin' but I bet it's that spicy rib-eye steak recipe with made-from-scratch bread and tossed salad. It is good stuff, Ricky."

"What time?"

"Between 5:30 and 6:00."

Ricky leaned back, the front legs of the chair raising several inches off the floor.

"Can I get back to you on that? I'm playing golf tomorrow afternoon and then I'm supposed to meet with my agent afterward. How about if I call you from the golf course tomorrow afternoon?"

"Sure."

Ricky saw a server bringing their food order over.

"Ummm, now that's smells good. I hope that's ours," said Al.

"It is, brother, it is," Ricky said.

Both men unfolded their napkins and placed them in their laps.

CHAPTER TEN

Lee Wyatt strolled down the canned-goods aisle of the Good Earth Food Mart. Deciding he had been eating out way more than his budget allowed, Lee wrote out a projected menu for his home-cooked meals for the next two weeks, looked up in two recipe books he'd purchased at the local book store yesterday what ingredients he'd need to prepare those meals, and then made his grocery list from that. His mission now was to find the pasta-ready sliced tomatoes for the spaghetti dinner he planned to make tomorrow night. A quarter of the way down the aisle, Lee saw a slender, attractive Native American woman approaching. She was attractive not only because of her perfect skin, long, thick ebony hair and perfectly sculpted facial features. An air of intelligence and compassion swirled about her. It was almost as if she had a halo above her head. Lee forced himself to look away. If he didn't, she might call store security to come take him away for sexual harassment or some such bullshit. So he grabbed two cans of the sliced tomatoes and crossed that item off his list.

"Are you using that to make spaghetti sauce?" the Native American woman asked.

"Yeah. Why?"

"Did you know if you add a few sprinkles of sugar, it'll make the sauce taste better?"

"Is that right?" he replied. "Why is that?"

"The sugar reduces the acidity of the tomatoes. Less acid, more tomatoey flavor," she replied.

"Hey, thank you very much. I'll try that," Lee said.

"You're new in town."

That definitely was not a question.

"That's right. I presume you are not new to Dying Tree," he said while wondering if this attractive woman struck up conversations with total strangers of the opposite sex on a regular basis.

"In some ways, I am fairly new to the town. I moved here a year and a half ago. But after moving here, I knew some part of me has been here before, maybe for a long time."

"Really? So you're a religious person then," Lee said.

"Spiritual but not religious. I believe and trust in forces I cannot directly detect with my conventional, ego-limited senses," she replied.

"I'm Lee Wyatt," he said while offering his hand.

"Naomi or Soaring Eagle. I'll answer to either one," she said while extending her hand.

"I like both of them. I think it's a great idea to have more than one name. That way other people have options for addressing you."

"Yes, this is quite true. I understand you work for Eileen out at the golf course," she said while maneuvering her cart to the side so another shopper could get by.

"Now how did you know that? Is this town that small and gossipy?"

Naomi/Soaring Eagle laughed, the silkiness of the sound gliding through the air like the animal for which she was named. The glow in her eyes grew a shade brighter when she laughed.

"I prefer to call Dying Tree 'well connected' or maybe 'efficiently networked'. Phrasing is everything. Or as an ancient Chinese philosopher and writer once said, 'Wisdom is knowing the proper names for things'."

"Which Chinese philosopher was that?" Lee asked.

"Wen Lu. Or maybe is was Lu Wen. I am not sure, to be honest with you."

"That's okay. It sounds poetic and wise so ultimately the source doesn't matter."

"You make an interesting point. One could argue there is a fundamental difference between the sage and the message of truth he or she delivers. The deliverer of the message and the message are very different from another, though I suspect the spirits of the great men and women of history are invariably interwoven with their messages of truth. Like Martin Luther King's soul is resurrected every time someone talks or thinks about the 'I have a dream' speech he is so famous for," said Naomi.

Another shopper, this one a mother with two young children, squeezed by them. The younger of the two children, a girl not more than six months, bellowed her unhappiness at being pushed around in a cart. Normally Lee would have been irritated but now he smiled and hoped, for the little girl's sake and that of her mother, that the crying fit ended soon. For the briefest of interludes, Lee could imagine being the mother of two young children.

"I see what you mean. It's like his ghost, which is of course no longer tied down to a physical body, can roam the universe as it seems fit. Naturally it would tend to migrate toward ideas and emotions expressed so eloquently by his old human, physical self. But then sometimes the messages delivered are different than the deliverers. Like when the senders of messages are eloquent hypocrites. I can't name specific examples but I'm sure that throughout history there've been alcoholic, child-molesting priests and preachers who've delivered knockout sermons on the power of God and the Holy Spirit and the redeeming power of the selfless love shown by his son, Jesus Christ. As they say, the truly righteous have no need of God. It's the sinners who get God's attention because they need the most help."

Suddenly the mundane aspects of food procurement seemed so petty. How could one concern themselves with buying ketchup when there were all these puzzling, intriguing mysteries of the universe to contemplate and solve? But then again, Lee mused, many armchair philosophers thought better after the hole in their stomach was sated with mac and cheese and a couple slices of bread. Or better yet, a pizza or steak.

"Well, I've truly enjoyed meeting you, Lee Wyatt, but I should finish up my little shopping expedition. However, if you'd like to continue this conversation later, I'd certainly be willing," she said.

"Sure, sounds good to me. Just name the time and place and I'll be there," he replied.

Naomi thought about it for ten seconds or so, then said, "What are you doing at midnight tonight?"

"Midnight?"

"It's the best time to contemplate such weighty matters. It's easier to invoke cosmic, timeless images when the land is covered with darkness."

"All right, I'll buy that. Now the question is: where?"

"Right outside the gates of Dying Tree Cemetery."

"Where's that?"

"Take Highway 36 just outside the west end of town. Get off on the first exit you see. Turn right after exit. Take another right at the next street. The graveyard sits on a hill halfway down that street. You can't miss it."

"I'll be there, Soaring Eagle."

"Good."

She smiled before pushing her cart down the canned goods aisle. Lee returned to his list and tried not to think about how much food he still had to buy.

*   *   *

Lee borrowed Frank's truck for the midnight rendezvous with Naomi. If his bicycle had a headlight, he would have rode it. But it didn't so he didn't. Now he employed conventional means to transport him to what he anticipated would be a most unconventional meeting. Given the time and place, how could it be otherwise?

He saw the exit Naomi alluded to. Lee flicked on the right turning signal and eased the Ford F-150 onto the off ramp. After waiting for a car to pass by, he took a right at the stop sign at the end of the ramp. The next street was Buffalo Run Avenue. He turned right and stayed in the right lane while looking for the cemetery turnoff. Two hundred yards later, he spotted a sign that read: DYING TREE CEMETERY—NEXT RIGHT.

As he eased up on the gas pedal, his heart rate jumped. Lee didn't know what he was so excited about. With a woman he'd just met who, though she was unquestionably attractive and friendly, was also so off-the-wall that it was impossible for him to predict what she might do. As the truck climbed the road that wound its way up the hill, Lee began to understand why he was so excited. It was precisely the thrill of not knowing what would happen that was exciting. Surprise birthday parties, surprise endings in movies and books, meeting someone new at school or work who made you think of ideas and possibilities you hadn't counted on encountering until the conversation began, unexpectedly hearing an owl calling out its nocturnal song right above you. All surprise moves in the chess game of life but all the more intriguing because of their sudden, surprising arrival.

He'd reached the top of the hill. A parking lot with perhaps thirty spaces lay directly in front of him. Beyond that, the locked wrought iron gates of the cemetery. As he'd expected, there were no vehicles occupying any of the other parking spaces. After all, who in their right mind would hang around a graveyard at this hour? But then Lee thought of Naomi. How did she get here? Lee maneuvered the truck into the space nearest the gates. It was marked for handicapped only but he was banking on the fact there'd be no handicapped mourners clamoring for the spot during the interval of time he'd be here.

After shutting off the lights and rolling up the windows, he hopped down from the truck. He locked up, double-checked the door on the driver's side—it was locked—and began searching for Soaring Eagle. The possibility that she was wouldn't show up darted across the horizon of his mental landscape but disappeared quickly. Though she seemed an unusual person, Naomi/Soaring Eagle struck Lee as honest and dependable. Though he had no prior experience to lean on as evidence, he just felt sure that his new-found acquaintance was true to her word. Perhaps it was the above-board, down-to-earth smile. Whatever the source for his gut feeling, he didn't question it. Onward he went, the gates of the cemetery growing larger in his eyes. He reached the bars, grasped hold, and peered between them in hopes of spotting her standing by one of the marble headstones.

No such luck. He dropped his hands from the bars down to his hips. Damn it, where was she?

"Looking for anyone in particular?"

He whirled around. The single sodium-vapor light in the parking lot, presumably on a timer, had gone out. Frank's truck was a vague outline as the cloudy sky blocked even the stars' attempts at illumination. Still, he should be able to see Naomi. She'd sounded near and the night wasn't that dark.

"Where in the hell are you?" Lee demanded of the night, disappointed that he'd had to ask the question.

"Right over here."

Now he knew where she had to be. A prodigious oak tree soared into the air, its trunk shooting up from the ground. It stood between the parking lot and the front gate. He'd noticed it but not given it more than a fleeting notice the first time he passed by. Drawing to within five feet of it, Lee saw Naomi snuggled up to tree's base, her right ear pressed to the oak's bark.

"What are you doing?" he asked.

She slowly leaned away from the trunk, her right ear no longer pressing against the old tree's skin. Naomi's eyes, so big and bright at the store, were even larger, though the shine in her eyes was different.

"I'm getting to know my friend a little better."

"The oak tree is your friend?" he asked.

"Of course. Why wouldn't it be? Oaks are so neat. They start off as such teeny tiny seeds but give them one or two hundred years and look what they become," she said reverentially, her gaze flowing up the tree's trunk toward the distant branches. "This one's seen a lot of changes since he's been born. Saw the prairie filled with bison, the Natives thriving on the land, then the arrival of the white settlers, the building of the town of Dying Tree around it."

She sighed, hesitated for a few seconds before continuing.

"Of course, it's seen a lot of people buried here. Much sorrow at first when the spirit leaves the individual body and returns to the Creator's plane but in the end, well, there is no end. That's the part a lot of people don't or maybe even can't understand. The cultures who live closer to the land, the ones labeled 'primitive' by the provincial Americans, they understand what's it's all about."

By now, Naomi had snuggled back up to the tree.

"Are you okay?" he asked.

"I'm fine," she replied. "I've been praying and meditating most of the night."

"Out here?" he asked.

"There's a nice spot in the forest alongside the western edge of the cemetery. No one knows I'm there. I went there right after I ate my heavenly meal, which was just after we met at the grocery store this afternoon."

"Heavenly meal?" he asked.

Naomi sat up, patted the oak tree much like a pet owner does with their beloved animal, and regarded Lee with a look that was intense but benign.

"Peyote."

"Really?" he said, "I've heard of it but never taken it. Isn't it like acid?"

Naomi rolled her eyes, laughed and said, "It's similar but I have to say, on this score, the Native American mind-altering practices are vastly superior to the white man's."

"Why is that?" Lee asked.

"Because peyote is natural and just as importantly, because of the rituals practiced before the spiritual food is taken. You see, true communion with the Creator can't be accomplished with mind-altering substances alone. How you prepare your heart, mind and spirit before digesting the substance is crucial. From my experiences, acid takers use little or no preparation. They buy the acid, tell a few of their friends, and get together, usually in someone's dorm room or at a frat house, maybe out in a forest or in a bar, and then take the stuff. Sure, they'll see a bunch of pretty and some not-so-pretty but fascinating hallucinations, laugh their asses off and feel profoundly enlightened and enthralled with the world during their trip. But then after they come down from the high, the odds are great they'll go on with their lives, pretty much the same as before the trip. The only time they'll feel so in touch with the universe and the Creator will be the next time they trip."

"So how's peyote and the Native American different?" he asked.

Soaring Eagle, now staring at the expansive branches of the oak tree, and maybe also at the night sky lingering behind the oak's limbs, said, "Remember this is a generalization and that not necessarily every native is so enlightened, but overall this is true: peyote practitioners' focus is not on the substance or the altered state itself. It's on what the experience reveals about how much reality is out there, within reach of our minds but buried under a morass of confusion, lies and preoccupation with petty, selfish concerns. Peyote, like human beings, is not an end unto itself. Its greatness lies in pointing us toward ultimate truth and reality."

"How does it do that?" Lee asked.

"One of the great truths I've learned is that words are inadequate to describe all aspects of the divine. You have to experience it to truly comprehend," she replied. "If you're interested, I have some left. I'd be happy to share the key to the door of Truth with you if you agree to perform the necessary rituals first. This is a sacred herb, not a street drug. They could not be more different. You must understand that from the outset."

"All right. I do see what you mean about preparing yourself. To me, the lack of rituals used by most acid trippers is reflective of a broader attitude of a capitalist, market-driven society. They think if they have enough money to buy enough of the right things at the right times, they will be happy. Their focus is on the material goods or services they'll receive. There's not much thought given to ritual or preparing their hearts or spirits. It's all about simply obtaining the right stuff and then wearing, playing with, riding in, eating or drinking it and then being happy with satisfying their needs and wants. There's little concern with how their actions affect the rest of the world. Even the ones who're bold enough to embark on mind-altering experiences tend to not do anymore work than they absolutely have to. They figure all they should have to do is find someone to sell them the drug, pay them for it, and then swallow it. The high will come and they'll have a great time. But they're missing out on so much because of their unwillingness to truly open up their mind. If they'd think stop and think about what their minds are truly capable of and what big questions they'd like to find answers for, they'd change and expand the very nature of the experience and in so doing, change themselves."

"Oh my god, that is exactly right! That's a little freaky, even for a veteran peyote user like myself. It was almost as if I was speaking directly through you," exclaimed Soaring Eagle. "Listen, I think you should try peyote. It won't change what you're capable of but it will drastically alter what you think you're capable of. Do you know what I mean?"

"In other words, it will open my ego-limited mind's eye so that I see how much I can truly do," he said.

"Exactly!"

"All right. So what rituals do I have to perform before I take the peyote?" he asked.

Soaring Eagle hopped to her feet, leaned over and planted a kiss on the oak tree's woody skin. "We've got to stop meeting like this," she whispered, then giggled for perhaps ten seconds. She took hold of Lee's right hand. "There's no one specific ritual you have to do. It differs for each person. Dancing, praying, meditating, any one of them is good. It could be as simple as just sitting quietly and contemplating where you're at and what the world is really like and how you think you could make the world—and thereby yourself because you're ultimately one and the same—happier."

"I understand. Let's see, I think a nice, long, contemplative walk through the graveyard would be the best thing. It seems I think better, more clearly, when I'm out walking around in a mostly natural environment. Like golf courses, for instance. Graveyards are very similar to golf courses, actually. You've got an outdoor setting, frequently on a hillside, that's carefully manicured and shaped by human hands as well as divine. It's a divine-man-made hybrid."

"All right, I see what you mean. That's very perceptive. Tell you what, you go do that and after you think you're ready to embark on a possibly divine journey into the depths of reality, where you may encounter the Creator, demon-spirits or possibly both, then return to this oak tree. I'll give you an hour or so."

"The problem is I'm not sure of the best way to get inside the graveyard. The front gate is obviously locked and I'm not crazy about the idea of scaling those bars," he said.

"If you walk around to the side nearest the highway and keep going to the rear of the graveyard, you'll find a spot where the land rises up seven or eight feet right outside the bars. At the highest point, all it takes is to reach up and grab the top of the bar and hoist yourself over," said Naomi.

"What about getting back out?"

"Oh you'll find a way somehow. I did. Of course, your way may not be the same as mine but that is all right. Whatever way works is the wisest."

"Meet back here in about an hour, right?" Lee asked.

"Yes," she replied.

"Do you have a watch?" he asked.

A smile beamed from her face.

"I'll use my internal, intuitive clock. When you're ready to begin the spiritual trek, I'll know it."

With that, they parted. While Lee went down the right side of the dead-space, Naomi slipped through the night into a congregation of trees on the left side. All around, the night and hillside watched eagerly.

*   *   *

Lee found the spot just as Soaring Eagle had described it. After landing unhurt on the short grass, he ambled all throughout the cemetery past a host of differently styled gravestones. They ranged from the modest, simple ones that were essentially nametags with the bookends of the birth and death years tacked on to ornate, towering pronouncements that read like marquees for the deceased. The latter included poetry and in two cases, full-fledged obituaries on marble. Common names like Anderson, Smith and Jones shared the space with Franzmeirs, Eides, and Sawmills. The better-known ones were located in the front-left corner overlooking the street. It was there that Frontier Billy McGee, Buffalo Rider Betty McCall, and Dance Hall Dinah had been buried so many years ago. What struck Lee most about the cemetery were all those great old oak trees. At first he thought it had been Naomi's work, the power of suggestion conspiring to inflate the trees' perceived value. But second and even third considerations brought him back to the same conclusion. Standing tall and spreading their arms so wide, they were like leafy, ultra-experienced bouncers, keeping watch over their sacred charges.

During the hour-long walk around and through the grounds of the dead, Lee struggled to prepare himself for the sacred journey Naomi spoke of. He'd heard plenty of stories from classmates while he was in college about drug experiences. A few almost freaked out but most of them highly recommended the experience. However, he had to agree with Naomi's contention that most acid takers failed to appreciate what was happening. Moreover, they probably were more fascinated with the mind-candy piece of the experience. For one night, they were different, but it didn't seem to change their lives. It was just another kind of high, more interestingly and memorable than pot or speed, but nothing revolutionary or truly enlightening. With Naomi and her peyote, the odds of something important coming from the experience seemed infinitely greater than the garden-variety acid trip.

He checked his watch. It'd been sixty-five minutes since he'd spoken with Soaring Eagle. Lee followed the winding cobblestone path toward the front gates. He still hadn't figured out how to get back out of the graveyard short of scaling the ten-foot bars. But like Soaring Eagle said, he'd find his way out somehow. This wasn't rocket science. Within three minutes, Lee strolled up to the gates. Naomi was there, her brown face plastered against the black bars.

"Am I the one imprisoned because I want to get in there so I can be closer to you or are you the prisoner because you're stuck inside the bars?" she asked, the painting of the sentence framed by the barest hint of laughter.

"I say neither one of us are prisoners because each of us knows we can go wherever we wish if only we exert enough effort and creativity. We're not prisoners, we're just mobilely challenged," Lee replied.

Naomi jumped back from the gate as if it suddenly became electrified. She poured out a spate of laughter, her face releasing the intellectual mask for several wonderful seconds. The laughter subsided but that wondrous smile remained as she again smushed her face up the bars.

"You're funny, oh great and powerful white man. Well, do you feel ready to begin the journey of a lifetime?"

"Bring it on, baby."

"This is serious. I meant what I said about being a sacred experience. I think you are smart enough and wise enough to realize your frame of mind is crucial. Have you ever taken any kind of hallucinogenic before?"

"Just pot and a little hashish," he replied. "But after hearing so many stories from old college buddies of mine, I feel like I've taken acid before."

"Let me give you a few words of advice. Don't be alarmed if you see something particularly frightening. My mantra is 'keep the flow going'. You may see or hear something that scares you. Just remember it won't last forever. It'll go away if you let it. Flow through the experience. Keep your consciousness flowing. If you do that, you'll never be overcome by any one image or sound," she said.

"Is it really going to be that intense?" Lee asked, more than trace of concern lacing his voice.

"It can be but it doesn't have to be. Remember that if you start with a happy, hopeful, positive state of mind, your odds of a bad experience are very small. Also remember I'm here if you need a hand to hold onto or just someone to talk to," Soaring Eagle said softly.

Lee expelled a long breath, closed his eyes while making the sign of the cross on his chest, opened his eyes and declared, "I'm as ready as I'll ever be."

As Soaring Eagle gave him the peyote, which resembled dried fruit in this musky light, she said, "It'll take about forty-five minutes, perhaps an hour, before you realize the sacred journey has begun."

"So what's going to happen?" Lee asked. "The trees and ground are going to start moving, right?"

"Perhaps. It is different for different people. The most important thing is to not try to predict what you will experience. Let your mind experience whatever happens. My philosophy with peyote is just like my general view of everyday life: bond with whatever happens to you. This means not entering the human race with a hidden agenda. When you do that, there is a tendency to not see things are they truly are but rather—"

"As you'd like to see them," finished Lee.

Soaring Eagle blessed him with another heart-melting smile.

"Precisely. The Creator is everywhere and in everything and everyone. The wise, astute mind perceives the spiritual reality inherent in all situations and acts accordingly. That means whether you encounter comedy or tragedy, there is something ultimately positive to be obtained from every experience. Peyote helps individuals see beyond their own little islands of self by putting them in touch with the deeper, more profound currents blowing through the universe."

Lee nodded, then said, "I'll buy that. So what's the proper ritual for actually eating these?"

"Find a place where you can sit comfortably. After you are seated, thank the Creator for the spiritual food you are about to eat and ask for guidance on the journey ahead," said Soaring Eagle.

Lee scanned the area. After a thorough review of the immediate terrain, he pointed to a spot on his right.

"I like that spot right over there."

She turned and saw that he was gesturing toward an oak tree ten feet away. Five feet away was a grave marked with a five-foot tall headstone with a cross crowning it.

"All right. While you do that, I will go around to the rear of the graveyard, climb over the fence and make my way over to you. You will have plenty of time to eat the holy meal so do not rush."

With that, she walked away, leaving Lee to himself and the peyote. He crossed over to the old oak and lowered himself to the ground. He got his knees into a semi-lotus position, bowed his head and thought of nothing for several seconds. After his breathing slowed, and the tempo of his mind did likewise, Lee opened his eyes. Silently he asked God to forgive all his sins and to bestow upon him the courage and wisdom on the trek ahead. Then he slowly brought the peyote to his mouth. For an instant, he considered backing out. *Just get up, give Soaring Eagle* back her drugs, and get the hell out of here. Return to the real world. Then he realized the real world was a lot more than just whatever his five senses could perceive. Whatever he experienced tonight was reality. It was just that it would be a deeper, different aspect of reality than he was used to.

Lee put the dried cactus tufts into his mouth and began chewing.

*   *   *

They strolled through Dying Tree Cemetery for thirty minutes, talking mostly about the implications of the personal computer revolution on humanity's spiritual development and then comparing the Native American Church's peyote use to the Buddhists' meditation practices. By the time Naomi finished explaining why she considered peyote superior to meditation, Lee was beginning to notice effects from the sacramental drug.

"Starting to feel something?" she asked.

A moment's hesitation, then he said, "Yeah, but I'm not sure exactly how to describe it." He took a few steps worth of reflection, then said, "It's almost like walking on the moon. I feel a lot lighter than normal, as if I could jump up in the air and not come back down for a long, long time. Or maybe it's more like the ground is less solid, as if the molecular structure of the grass and dirt has been fundamentally changed. Whatever the cause, I like it. I feel like Tigger from Winnie the Pooh."

"Bouncin'?" Naomi said in her best Tigger voice.

Lee smiled.

"T-I—double GERR," he shouted out before breaking into a fit of laughter.

"Bouncin' would be fun. Everyone should do some kind of bouncing everyday—trampolines or bungee jumps, whatever it takes to get yourself bouncin'," said Soaring Eagle.

"But bouncin' isn't necessary for happiness," began Lee, "I mean just look at Pooh bear. He never bounced a day in his life, at least not in the episodes I've seen, and he's gets along great. Just so long as he has his jars of honey, he's one happy, roly-poly bear," Lee said with such seriousness.

"That's a dangerous way of thinking."

"Oh?"

"Yes because you're assuming Pooh won't ever change. Maybe the television people will decide to create a made-for-TV movie where Pooh goes on a new diet that limits, or dare I say it, excludes any honey."

Lee fixed her with an expression usually reserved for people whose wardrobe featured a large selection of coats that tied at the back.

"That is unthinkable," he intoned.

"Like the Titanic was unsinkable," said Soaring Eagle.

Lee hopped off the winding cobblestone path they'd been on. He plopped himself down at the base of a birch tree, its ghostly skin gleaming in the starlight. He folded his left arm across his stomach, stuck his right elbow on top of his left wrist, and put his right hand to the right side of his face. His right index finger tapped on his right-hand cheek.

"Think, think, think . . . yeah, it's possible that could happen, I guess. It'd never happen, I would venture to say, but it's possible. I guess it's like envisioning Norm from Cheers on the wagon. Or Norm being skinny or ambitious."

"Who's Norm and what's Cheers?"

"You've never seen the show?" Lee asked incredulously.

"No. My television viewing is limited to news, the history channel, and public television."

"Not very open-minded when it comes to TV, are we?"

"No, I guess I'm too busy exploring life in more direct, honest ways. I think television is a lot like the old-fashioned bubble gum. It tastes good but it slowly rots whatever it touches. Why rely on a third-person with his or her own views to entertain and inform you? To me, the more direct an experience is, the more authentic and fulfilling it is. Television is just too much of a filtered process. Add to that the fact your mind can ease into cruise control too often. To take the metaphor one step farther, you could say TV not only rots what it touches, it promotes laziness, which causes mental atrophy."

"Wow, that's deep," said Lee. After several heartbeats of reflection, he hopped up to his feet. "All right, let's keep going with the dead-space tour, shall we?"

"Keep moving but not rushing, I say," said Soaring Eagle.

At that moment, with the peyote having had nearly an hour to work its magic on him, Lee could easily imagine Naomi becoming a real soaring eagle. As light as he himself felt, it was easy to bestow that airy feeling onto his new friend. The problem with the image was that he couldn't imagine Naomi swooping down from the sky to snatch up prey. She seemed much too nice and gentle to be a hunter. Then Lee laughed as he pictured Naomi as an eagle sitting at table with a red and white checkered cloth over it. The eagle was eating a bowl of pasta with a meatless sauce because she couldn't bear to kill prey for her survival. Garlic bread and a salad rounded out the envisioned meal. A quick tour of the rest of the imaginary restaurant scene revealed a threesome of male lions devouring freshly killed meat at one table with the neighboring table full of hyenas waiting to see if there'd be any leftovers for them. The table next to the hyenas had an elephant squeezed into giant chair, a heap of unshelled peanuts piled on a platter in front of it. A smoking cigar lay in an ashtray just to the right of the peanut entree. Behind the elephant was a gorilla with a Samsonite suitcase full of bananas. The luggage was on its back and the top swung up to allow easy access to the store of yellow fruit. Rounding out the wildlife dinner was a shark reading a newspaper at a table that was essentially a swimming pool. Inside the table-swimming pool were three men and three women, all swimming at the water's surface with shark fins protruding from their backs. Despite his best efforts to block it out, the theme music from "Jaws" played to an ever-sharpening climax as the shark set down the newspaper and began choosing which one of the swimmers he wanted to eat first.

"Imagining something amusing?" asked Soaring Eagle.

"Is it that obvious?" Lee replied.

"Yes. Believe me, I had similar experiences on my earlier journeys. As you become more versed in traveling the heavenly path, the frequency of the silly, inane images decreases."

"Oh, that's unfortunate. It seems to me humor is one of God's greatest gifts."

"I suppose so. Laughter is the best medicine for what ails you, that sort of thing. Well, you will have moments of great humor while on the pathway. It is just that their frequency declines somewhat as you get more used to the higher state," said Soaring Eagle.

They'd reached the northwest corner of the graveyard. Down below them, between the iron bars, they could see the street. To the left was the traffic light. Lee became transfixed with the way the circles of light appeared. The red light was no longer just a sphere. The peyote's invisible hand had painted eyelashes all around the circumference of it. On a normal eye, it would have appeared ungainly. In this case, it seemed perfectly normal. But of course normal wasn't the right word. Lee was feeling anything but normal. Then it occurred to him, really hitting him, that normal was such a facade. Average, acceptable, normal—those terms had no permanent relevancy because there were so many different conceptions of what they were. It varied so radically across different cultures. And besides, what was wonderful about being normal anyway? Labeling an individual as normal was in essence robbing a person of their uniqueness.

Who needed that?

The insight was a flash of lightning in the night sky of his mind. Though violent and illuminating, it was over in an instant. Suddenly he was aware of how the very air through which he moved was rife with an otherworldly energy. What acted like a low-grade electricity pulsed through the air, sending tiny, not-quite-painful shocks over every square inch of his body. No surface portion of his body was exempt from the tingly sensation. It was as if the cemetery was a giant aura field through which he moved. Every step he took propelled him through this field, the aura in the air coating his body as he passed through. Lee likened it to swimming. The aura was like water. As one swam through it, the motion of the swimmer caused waves that rippled through the water for a short while before dissipating.

"Are you all right?" she asked.

"Never better. The air seems charged, doesn't it?" he said.

"If it seems so to you, then it is. It was more tangible for me earlier in the evening but I still feel it. It stems largely from the intense feelings, mostly grief, that have been experienced in this space over the decades. It's an aspect of reality our ego-laden, narrow minds normally fail to appreciate. That all changes when you travel the sacred path. You perceive aspects of the universe normally veiled."

Lee nodded.

"What about other energy forms? It's like maybe the spirits of the dead returning to check out their old containers or vessels. I don't know, kind of like for old time's sake, I suppose."

"Unquestionably. Most cultures believe, and rightly so, that the spirits of the dead, right after death, remain close to the body. The spirit or soul of the deceased is theorized to be unsure how to reach high planes so it hangs around the most familiar thing it knows: its body and close friends and relatives who attend the funeral. After the grieving period is past, the soul migrates, either because it summons the courage to explore the ultimate unknown or grows bored and weary of hanging around the graveyard. Probably some of both."

Lee considered that as he scanned the marble monuments they passed by. Since reaching the northwest corner of the graveyard, the two had made slow but steady progress. They were almost to the very back of the cemetery, the street, like a stream, flowing along below them on the left, the rows of graves on their right. Soaring Eagle walked closest to the fence while Lee had the inside track. He suddenly altered course. Now instead of three feet separating the two, they were shoulder to shoulder.

"What's wrong?" she asked.

"They're touching me."

"The spirits?" she asked.

He nodded. The sensation of swimming through the air was pleasant earlier but now it felt more like drowning in a sea of zombies. They were supposed to be dead but a misshapen, warped, ungodly life force coursed through the legions of dead, leaving them grotesque but still eager to explore any poor living souls who were unfortunate enough to swim nearby. Their octopus-like tentacles threatened to wrap around him and reel him into the fold. Lee felt the force trying to draw him closer to something he was entirely already near enough to. His lungs and mouth had trouble getting air. It was like the air was mostly water and he was slowly drowning.

Soaring Eagle must have seen the expression on his face or perhaps sensed his discomfiture. She wrapped her right hand in his left.

"Remember: KEEP THE FLOW GOING. You'll get through this. Whatever you believe is out there is really inside your mind. The peyote only makes more real whatever your deepest thoughts are. Change the source, the true origins of your thoughts, and you change the nature of your perceptions. It's a classical example of the ultimate truth of self-fulfilling prophecies. Believe it and it will come true. Lee, are you listening to me?"

There was a slight hesitation as he continued staring toward the graves.

"I said, are you listening to you?" in a voice just beneath a shout as she pinched the fleshy part on the back of Lee's upper arm.

"Ouch! Damn it, yes, I'm listening," he said irritably. After seeing his friend's gentle, warm face, the irritation quickly flew away.

Relief settled over the landscape of his face. He smiled. "Thanks. Boy, did I need that. For a second there, the water was getting really choppy."

"But now your ship has found a calm bay to dock in?" offered Soaring Eagle.

Lee paused, cast a visual net over the network of graves and the waves of energy buzzing from and through the space. Two of the headstones had flickering images, presumably of the deceased lying below, peering out from the rectangles of marble. An instant later, one of the images had transformed back into the engraving normally found on the headstones while the other one, though still there, grew less distinct. It was then that

Lee found he could hear his blood running through his veins. Shortly after that, he heard what must be God (the Creator in Soaring Eagle's words) breathing. Or was it the sap running through the innards of the trees', now his friends, except maybe for the one oak in by the gates whose long branches pushed him away instead of hugging him like the rest? Then he realized it was all the same. Instead of the localized image he'd always presumed God to be, Lee realized at that precise moment of incredible, blinding insight how woefully inaccurate and provincial that conception of the Creator was. With his senses endowed with awesome, transcendent power, he saw with a clarity he hadn't ever experienced before the great currents of seething, spiritual, quantum energy blowing through the world. Names and histories of people were just props, not lasting truths. A drunken degenerate in the morning could be an evangelist by the time night fell. Cripples one day might be healed by the next. Poor, restless youths could be gang members one moment, youth leaders in churches the next. And of course it went the other way too. Men who'd risen to the pinnacle of society—presidents, army generals, CEO's of multinational corporations, preachers with sometimes millions of followers—dropped from their lofty perches. The old Achilles' heels, traps present since humans rose from apes, hungrily gathered them in. Extra-marital sex, drugs, lust for more power, and greed lurked for the loosely tethered, unfocused leaders of society. With the power and raw numbers of the media, the downfalls of such people were chronicled with excruciating accuracy and detail. If those figures' meteoric rise to the top was steeped with a healthy mysticism, their subsequent fall was decidedly not. Videotapes, tape recordings, Web sites oozing with data and photographs, television channels for every eclectic interest known to mankind that broadcast around the clock, and radio stations, probably broadcast over the Internet, had validated earlier fears of Big Brother always watching. It was, Lee mused, the downside of being connected with folks who couldn't empathize with one another. A global village didn't necessarily get along with one another but they sure the hell knew what everyone else was up to.

Suddenly Lee realized they'd stopped moving. Even before he tore his gaze from the graves, he felt Naomi (she'd landed, at least for now, Lee decided, so it was right to think of her as Naomi) staring at him.

"Quarter for your thoughts?" she said.

"Let me guess, inflation," he answered.

"That is right. So, tell what you were thinking and I'll owe you the quarter, all right?"

They'd begun walking again, this time along the cemetery's rear boundary. The waves of malevolent force from the dead had eased sufficiently to allow Lee to continue his current inside track. A roar like a dragon or dinosaur pierced the relative peace. The sound invaded the space all around them. Lee jumped back, his left shoulder bouncing off Naomi's right shoulder and brushing against her right breast. Fright overrode any libidinous feelings that might have developed.

"What in the hell was that?" he asked her.

"Do not worry. That must have been a semi from the highway. I heard but it not with the intensity you did. I went through that earlier tonight, only back then it was an owl. It sounded like there was one in every tree around here and each one had a megaphone in front of its mouth. That was interesting. I remember thinking it was like a being interrogated by the Spanish Inquisition back in the 16th century. They were all demanding to know 'who', who', who' . . ."

Naomi had given way to Soaring Eagle, the laughter and smiling lifting her spirits so dramatically that Lee was waiting for his companion to lift off the ground. They'd covered three-quarters of the rear fence. A frown marred Lee's face.

"What's wrong?" Soaring Eagle asked.

"Wasn't there a question you'd asked a little while ago but I didn't answer it because of the invasion of the sound?" he answered.

She paused, then said, "Umm, yes, you are right about that, but I cannot think of the question right at the moment."

Soaring Eagle's expression contracted, her eyes not straying from the path directly in front of her. She strained to recall what the question had been. Then she stopped walking completely. A half-second later, she began walking backwards. Lee stared unabashedly at her.

"What in the hell do you think you're doing?" he demanded.

"I'm trying to recreate the scene when I asked you the question," she said while continuing her reverse motion. Lee chuckled as he followed her movements back to a spot twenty-five yards away. He watched Soaring Eagle shut both eyes. Perhaps a minute later she spoke.

"I know what it was," she announced triumphantly, "I asked you what you were thinking of because you had a queer expression on your face. I was very curious about what exactly you were thinking."

Lee paused and then said, "At the time, my mind was filled with a boggling array of thoughts. I got started on an idea and kept going and going with it. I guess the length of the thread I wove surprised me. It was like I'd rambled on so much that I amused myself."

"What were you thinking about?" Soaring Eagle wanted to know.

He spread his hands wide, shaking his head all the while.

"It's hard to put into words. I don't know where to begin."

They kept walking. The northeastern corner of the cemetery waited only twenty yards beyond their current heading.

"I have what I immodestly think of as a splendid idea," announced Soaring Eagle.

"What?" he asked excitedly.

"I think we should build ourselves a fire. Then can we sit down, relax, and you can take as much time as you feel you need to tell me about your thoughts. How does that sound?"

"Wonderful. Do you have any matches to light the fire?" he asked.

"Yes, I do," she said.

"Do you smoke cigarettes?"

"No. Just grass once in a great, great while."

"Really?"

"Really. Does that surprise you?" she asked.

"No, I guess not," he managed. "Okay, let's build a fire. Where's a good spot?"

Soaring Eagle took several seconds, and then said, "Right over there."

Lee followed the invisible path her right index finger indicated. The spot she pointed to was in the very rear corner of the graveyard. One of the oak patrol stood only five feet away, the broad trunk shooting straight up, its myriad gnarled branches extending beyond the confines of the graveyard.

"Seems like as good a place as any," he said. He was going to ask what they were going to use to make the fire but caught himself before asking the stupid question. They'd use tree limbs and sticks, something human beings—and cavemen and cavewomen, for that matter—had used throughout the millennia. Several minutes later, having built up a pile at least three feet high, they rested. Soaring Eagle bent over, struck a match, and set the flame to the collection of wood scraps. The yellow flame climbed the pile, quickly reaching the pinnacle. Before he could help himself, Lee was peering into the depth of the flames. Never had he witnessed a fire more alive. He let the flickering, random beat of the flames draw his attention to it, an invisible but powerful bond between the fire and himself forming as he watched and listened to the uneven crackling and popping of the fire.

Without his realizing it, the rest of his surroundings melted away from his awareness, as if the fire were so hot it melted whatever or whomever was not entranced by its fiery depths. For him, the only reality was the writhing flames, leaping up to nip at the night air. He considered looking away to investigate a sound that seemed to originate on the highway but resisted. Once his concentration settled upon the fire, it was happy to stay there. Though earlier he'd found it difficult to concentrate on anything for more than ten or twenty seconds, now Lee found it difficult, once his consciousness alit upon an object, person or idea, to stop concentrating on it. Everyone and everything had more dimensions and aspects to them. No, that wasn't right. Now, aided by the peyote, he directly perceived not only all the different aspects of creation, he appreciated and understood, in an abstract manner, how all those different aspects worked together. Still, there were concepts there he didn't completely understand the mechanics of.

Allowing the curiosity to simmer in his psychological stewpot, he shifted his attention back to the primordial concentration of fiery energy. He felt in some respects like a man at a strip show, seated here, peering at the fire, watching the flames perform their steamy, sensuous dance against the black backdrop of the night sky. There was no need to slip a one or five into this dancer's G-string, however. This exotic dancer needed no motivation to continue the show. It burned because it had to and whatever fascination it provided for onlookers was entirely peripheral.

The crackling and hissing from the fire sounded normal one moment, ungodly loud the next. Moreover, there was a definitive rhythm to the different intensities. It was like a loop in a computer software program or more poetically, the circle of life and death.

Listening to the sounds more closely, Lee found if he used the razor's edge of focused concentration, he could control the pace of the flames' sound loop. Instead of the sound level switching from normal to loud every three second or four seconds as it had before, Lee first slowed it down so he perceived the different levels for ten-second intervals, then he sped up the loop so that loud and normal were heard in only one-second intervals.

"Controlling the differing sound levels of the fire?" Soaring Eagle asked.

Lee jerked around to face her. It'd felt like his new friend had lifted up the top of his skull and peeked at the thoughts parading around in their underwear.

"It's another latent aspect of our being brought to the surface by the peyote. Over the years, I have found it carries over, to a degree, to my normal, everyday life," she said.

Lee continued staring at her while slowly shaking his head.

"You are something else. I've never encountered anyone quite like you before, at least not on a personal level," he said.

"Really?"

"Really."

He waited for her to press him to explain whether he meant that as a compliment, criticism, or both. That she did not say anything said volumes about her. Soaring Eagle flew through life the way she was without waiting for permission or approval from anyone.

They both fell silent. The incessant shifting and cackling made the fire like a hyperactive witch. After a timeless interval, Lee's inner dialogue died down. He no longer felt compelled to form words in his mind that described what he perceived. The quiet in his mind let him completely, truly bond with the fire's pure essence. Not only did he perceive and appreciate the details and intricate patterns in the fire in front of them, he began comprehending the various aspects of significance of the concept of fire. It was a physical tool to combat extreme cold, a method of converting raw meat into civilized sustenance, a method of ignition for countless types of machinery such as car engines, and fire was a symbol of purity and Hell. But Lee perceived those different aspects in a visual rather than word-laden language.

At some point, Lee's peyote-fueled consciousness stumbled across a plane of existence that allowed effortless travel back and forth through time. He'd become so accustomed to the peyote's powers of expanded perceptions that he didn't try to deny the truth of his entrance to the new realm. He simply kept his mind pointed toward the truth of whatever he was discovering. Though the actual physical fire was still five feet away, the same as when he'd sat down, in his mind, it was pushed back four or five times that distance. The seemingly greater gap provided adequate room for the players in a newly forming drama. Images of Neanderthal and Cro-Magnon men and women appeared between him and the fire for a few seconds before flying off to the north, south, east, and west corners of the fire. The fire returned to its previous spot five feet in front of him. Lee briefly wondered if the peyote had driven him crazy but decided that as long as he realized what he was seeing wasn't happening in what he'd come to consider the "normal" world, and then he was okay. He was just conventionally challenged, which was all right.

After passing the sanity test, Lee found his point-of-view had changed. Now he wasn't watching one of the four cave people sitting around the fire. He was one of them. Sitting at the fire opposite of the curious looking guy with fairer skin and much less hair than himself and wearing the strangest looking clothing, Lee stared at the flames with new eyes and a different mindset. For now, he'd forgotten he knew the history of fire and its effect on the long parade of human beings who'd used and died from it. He was able to watch the fire much like the first human beings did, with a fascination born of curiosity, fear and healthy superstition. Then the four cave people, three women and one man, were drawn back into the fire, the representations of bodies having morphed into streams of fire that merged with the flames. The moment they merged with the fire, Lee's consciousness leapt back into his body. His heart sounded as if it were trying to beat hard enough to burst through his chest, like it was being chased by something so gruesome that it had to escape the confines of his body no matter the cost. From a distant place, he felt a gentle hand alit on his right wrist.

"You will be fine. Come, tell me about your journey and then I will tell about mine," offered Soaring Eagle.

He did and she did. They talked for over an hour. Halfway through her story, Soaring Eagle stopped so she could replenish the fire, then finished relating her experiences. While Lee's was rife with more vivid, concrete hallucinations, hers was more subtle though no less profound. She reflected on everyday events and people and ways of living and thinking that would help make the world happier. She saw with blinding clarity how simple, in theory, it was to live a happy life that made others around her happier because of her thoughts and acts. Her experience certainly wasn't devoid of the more concrete glimpses into the deeper realities. She'd seen and heard the cosmic, multi-layered winds of primordial power blow through and around them, the event like a handshake from God or she called it, the Creator.

Sunrise was only two hours away. Earlier Soaring Eagle had mentioned to Lee that the caretaker for the cemetery liked to get an early start, usually beginning work by seven o'clock to prep the place so it was ready to open by eight. With the historical figures buried here, it was important to have the grounds neat and clean for all the tourists. Having said that, the two agreed they'd leave the cemetery by six o'clock, six-fifteen at the latest. Budgeting for ten minutes of clean-up and cover-up, that left a little under ninety minutes of exploration time here at the cemetery.

"I'm curious about how exactly this stuff works," Lee said while peering at the dwindling fire.

"There are essentially two theories, the scientific and the occult," Naomi replied, the soaring eagle having landed on the firm ground of logic and reason.

"I think I can guess which camp you fall into," he said.

She shook her head.

"No, I bet you cannot."

"You believe in the scientific theory!? No fricking way."

Another shake of her head was followed by a knowing smile.

"I believe both theories have merit and that the two are not mutually exclusive. You see, the scientific theory says that a hallucinogenic like peyote disguises itself as a neurotransmitter—"

"Hold on there, what in the hell is a neurotransmitter?" Lee asked. He had a hazy idea but that was all.

"First off, brain cells are called neurons."

"That much I knew," Lee offered.

"All right, very good. So then, how do you think neurons communicate with one another?" Naomi asked.

"Hell, I don't know, telephones?"

She frowned at him.

He shrugged before saying, "Pagers? E-mail? A nudge in the ribs? Notes sent by homing pigeons?"

Naomi shook her head and then looked away. She fell silent.

"I'm sorry. I didn't know so I was trying to gloss over my ignorance with a layer of humor. I really do want to know."

Naomi slowly found his gaze again.

"All right, anyway, neurons communicate with electricity. What happens is an electrical impulse buzzes down the length of the first neuron. When it reaches the end of it, which is very close but not quite touching another neuron, it still needs to cross a tiny gap between the neurons. This gap is called a synapse. Are you with me so far?"

"Electricity . . . down the length of neuron . . . tiny valley called synapse separates communication. Yeah, I think I got it."

"Good. All right, now is where neurotransmitters come into play. In order for the electrical impulse to cross over that gap and reach the second neuron, it generates a neurotransmitter, which is like a hot-air balloon that the impulse hops into. It then flies across to the other side. This completes the communication process. A thought in the unconscious part the brain has been dispatched to the conscious part via electricity."

"Wow, that is wild! But how does the peyote create hallucinations?"

"The chemical structure of a hallucinogenic like peyote looks very similar to neurotransmitters—"

"Oh yeah, that's what you said earlier," Lee piped in.

"Right. Anyway, because the peyote tricks the mind into thinking there are all these extra neurotransmitters, impulses or ideas that normally would not reach the hallowed land of our consciousness do indeed reach our awareness. Under normal circumstances, the bizarre, hallucinogenic effects would not be present because they'd be filtered out."

"So really the peyote is like a counterfeit passer of hot-air balloons. Instead of passing fake tens or twenties, it passes fake neurotransmitters, which are basically hot-air balloons that carry electricity in the brain from one neuron to the next," said Lee.

"Right."

"And hallucinations are the passengers on those artificially created balloons."

"Right again," said Naomi. "That's very good."

Lee nodded smugly and then said, "So now we're left with the occult explanation of peyote."

"Right. Well, now is where it gets more complicated," she said.

"More complicated? Hell, we already have neurons, electricity, impulses, synapses, neurotransmitters and inept filters. How can the occult theory be more complicated?" he said incredulously.

Naomi glanced away for several seconds, then turned back to catch Lee's gaze.

"The occult theory involves the effects of the drugs on the seven chakras. In addition, there are four types of bodies as well."

"Yikes. Maybe I need to take notes," he grumbled.

"No, nothing like that. It's not necessary to memorize the chakras or the way peyote and similar drugs affect all of them. You just have to comprehend the general idea, the underlying principle that explains what happens on the mystical path through heaven and occasionally hell. Just remember to think big picture, all right?"

He nodded.

"First let's begin with the most fundamental part of occult theory. Occultists say our consciousness is independent from our body. That differs from science, which states the brain is the source of our consciousness. They can't explain how that can be, which is a big strike against them. But I digress. All right, occultists also say there are three more worlds, which they call 'planes', in addition to the physical one. Astral or emotional is one, mental is another, and buddhic or soul is yet another. There are bodies for each of these. That means we have an astral, buddhic, mental and physical body. So right from the beginning, they don't claim our physical body is responsible for our mental state, which makes sense to me."

"I agree," said Lee.

"The seven chakras, which are energy channels between the different planes, are affected when peyote is taken. There are physical sites on the body, for example, the navel, heart and top of the head are three of the seven chakras. However, there are psychological states tied to these spots. For instance, the spiritual is tied with the top of the head and empathy is part of the heart chakra."

"Makes sense," Lee said, his eyes now on Naomi instead of the fire. Somehow it seemed more important to see the speaker's face now that more technical matters were on the table of discussion. But he still felt the tongues of the fire's flames lapping at him, eagerly vying for his attention. "I mean, that ties in with all the expressions about having a heart, he or she has a big heart, home is where the heart is, and then of course there is Hart to Hart."

He laughed but of course his selective-television-viewing friend didn't. She smiled and let Lee's one-man joke be taken away from the discussion table like a dirty dish.

"As I was saying, it's the effect on the energy channeling centers of ourselves that are affected when peyote is taken. For example, one of the things that usually happens during a spiritual trek aided by peyote, something you obviously experienced because you described it to me, are visual hallucinations."

"Big time," he said.

"Now you remember how scientists would explain this, right?" she asked.

"Oh great, another damn pop quiz. I thought I'd left those behind in college. Well, let's see, don't tell me. I'll get this one, I really will. They'd say it's unfiltered visual phenomenon, static in the brain, ah, let's see . . . it's a balloon thing. Oh yeah, the hallucinations are passengers that rode over in fake hot-air balloons over the valleys of neighboring neurons."

Naomi beamed a smile that in earlier times would have said to launch a thousand ships.

"Actually most scientists wouldn't have quite been quite that poetic but essentially, you're right. The significance of the visual hallucinations in scientific circles is downplayed. They're reduced to tricks our minds play on us. It's as if the peyote is the devil who puts ideas in our brain's cells to play tricks on their neighbors."

"It doesn't feel that way to me. I bet most of those scientists haven't actually, as you say, 'embarked on a heavenly journey'. If they would have, they'd probably change their views," he said.

"I agree. Now, are you ready for the occult explanation of the visual hallucinations?" she asked.

Lee nodded vigorously. He began licking his chops in anticipation of the intellectual dish before him. Now it was up to Naomi to take the silver cover off the entree.

"You are funny. All right, occultists explain the hallucinations by saying the peyote stimulates the third eye—"

"Hold it, where's the third eye? Have we discussed this yet?" Lee broke in.

"I am sorry. We have not. The third eye is . . ." she paused while pointing at her own forehead, right between and just above her eyes " . . . right here, in the middle of the forehead. The third-eye chakra is associated with sight, cognition and clairvoyance. Clairvoyance is perception of adjacent planes, which is what you experienced tonight. Does any of that make sense?"

"Oh yes, a helluva lot of sense. I've heard most of the terms you've used but never before has someone tied it all together in a coherent theory. That is interesting," he said, his gaze traveling away from Naomi toward the fire and the tombstones beyond. Somewhere a bird shrieked. It sounded like a soul trapped in purgatory, begging for help or at least to be put out of their misery.

"What about audio hallucinations?" he heard himself asking.

"Stimulation of the throat chakra," she replied.

"Throat?" he frowned.

She used both hands to point at her throat and then slowly traced lines outward until each index finger touched an earlobe.

"The throat chakra is responsible for speech, hearing and clairaudience. The last one is perception of sounds on adjacent planes," she explained.

"All right, the picture is growing more complete. It's like those paint-by-number kits only the pieces aren't so cut and dried. More complex but also infinitely more interesting," he said.

She frowned at him.

"What are paint-by-number kits?"

He waved away the explanation.

"Never mind. It's not important. Just another toy invented for the masses' enjoyment."

"That does not sound so bad," said Naomi.

"Oh it's not harmful, I suppose, but anyway, I am starting to understand. The most interesting thing is the implications for the rest of our lives. I mean like you say, the most important part of the experience isn't the wild, fascinating, otherworldly things you perceive while on the mystical road of peyote. It's the deeper, largely unseen dimensions that are out there all the time, that are forgotten by most people most of the time. Out of sight, out of mind. But the peyote trips highlight the vastness and depth of the universe. It's like peeking between the slats and seeing Heaven and Hell."

"And countless things in-between," she said. Now she was Soaring Eagle again, the twinkle in her eyes and mystical smile sending her aloft in the skies of the universal mind, of which Lee was always a part of but rarely appreciated. Now he did appreciate it. The line from Shakespeare about the world being a stage and everyone merely players never seemed truer. One moment we're one person in a certain role, the next we're something completely different.

"We should start cleaning up. The caretaker will be here soon," he said.

"There is still time to explore," she replied.

"I think I've explored this little tract of the universe long enough. It's time to explore other spaces. Call me paranoid but I don't want to take any chances with being caught. I've got Frank's truck so his name would find its way into any police report that's filed."

"All right. Let's clean up and get outta Dodge."

*   *   *

Eleven o'clock. The peyote, though it hadn't completely run its course, was nearing the end. There wasn't a lot of steam left in the spiritual food's locomotive, though it still chugged along the cosmic, mystical tracks of his mind. The audio and visual hallucinations, increase in abstract reasoning ability and sensation of his very body being lighter and nearly transparent had receded into memory. Sitting here in front of the television set in his free room above the clubhouse of the Crazy Horse Golf Club, Lee felt close enough to being straight that he could trust his judgment on the really important issues in this experience called life. As he leaned back in the fake leather recliner, Lee tried to make sense of what he'd just been through. The volume on the TV set was muted to make introspection and contemplation easier.

Soaring Eagle and he had moved the truck three blocks from the cemetery. She knew of a cave just a block from they parked the truck. With her leading the way up a hillside, they picked their way through a tangle of brush and thick trees until reaching the cave. Once inside it, they made another fire. The shadows wiggling and dancing on the walls assumed what seemed like a thousand different shapes and identities. Again the illusion of traveling back to prehistoric times beckoned, though the second time the intensity of the mind trick had lessened. Soaring Eagle and he spoke of many things, but mostly it was of their respective childhoods. The bulk of it was their religious upbringing. Lee was a nice little Lutheran while Soaring Eagle was raised in the traditional Native American way. That conversation had wound down after two and a half hours. From there, after extinguishing the fire and cleaning up after themselves, the two ate breakfast at Norma Jean's Kitchen Nook. Lee wasn't particularly hungry when Naomi first broached the subject. His appetite magically appeared shortly after they'd stepped through the door. The sights and aromas of steaming plates full of eggs, pancakes and French toast served to remind his stomach of how long it'd been since he ate a meal of any considerable substance. It was three days since he ate more than a sandwich and a few chips at any one sitting. The skillet breakfast he ordered was just the ticket.

While Naomi ate at an even pace, chewing her food thoroughly and methodically, Lee ravaged the multi-layered mound of hash browns, eggs and bacon strips. The slices of toast were swallowed up within four bites per slice. He washed it down with a glass of ice water and large orange juice. Though he didn't roll out of the restaurant, he walked more slowly than he did into the place.

Lee drove her home. As they sat inside the truck's cab, he thanked Naomi several times for opening his senses to the infinite and his place inside that heavenly, mysterious framework. She smiled, leaned over, and hugged him. Then suddenly, just before her hand grasped the door handle, he touched her left wrist with his right hand.

"I am curious about one more thing," he said,

"What is that?" she said.

"Why me?"

"You mean why did I ask an almost total stranger to meet me at a graveyard at midnight, then offer him a powerful mind-changing substance, all the while exchanging much personal information and opinions on a vast array of subjects?"

"Exactly."

"It was an instinctive feeling, one that bypassed logic and reason altogether. I wanted to know you better. After I got to know you a little better, I liked you enough to want to help you understand the unity and tremendous freedom of the universe. And it wasn't just personal reasons either. There was something, maybe an aura I sensed rather than saw, surrounding you. The aura meant you were special, someone who wasn't just passing through our little town for a mere sightseeing tour or to find a job for a few months while you earned just enough money to leave the area. I got the impression you very well might have a huge impact on Dying Tree."

"You're kidding? What kind of impact could I make?" he asked.

"That's the thing of it. I have no idea. On the face of it, not much. You are an assistant greens keeper at a golf club; you like to play pool and drink several cold beers once, maybe twice a week; you borrow a friend's truck to get around at night; and you hang around with native girls in graveyards. Hmm, that does not sound very promising, does it?" she said through a smile.

Though words themselves implied he wasn't anything special, her expression and tone said otherwise. Soaring Eagle was again aloft, her message rife with irony, her soul layered with contradictions. She thought he truly was special but it was his spirit, his inner self, not the worldly suit he wore to his job or showed to his friends and local tavern personnel.

"Will we, ah, get together again in the near future?" he asked.

"Do you mean a date?" she asked back.

"Yeah."

She considered the question and eventually said, "No."

Lee's shoulders and head, and of course his spirits, collectively sagged. Soaring Eagle shot out both hands to take hold of his.

"Do not take it as a rejection. I did not intend it that way at all. It is just the way I am. The time is not right for me to develop a serious relationship with any man. Relationships like those demand more of a commitment of emotion and energy that I can spare. Right now, I am still struggling with the true nature of things. Before I choose a life-long mate and kindred spirit, I need to understand the world's soul better. My inner journey has just begun. I would be cheating any potential mate because I would be too preoccupied with my spiritual, intellectual quest."

"But aren't intense personal relationships part of the inner journey?" he said.

"They can be. It is different for different people. For myself, I need to soar through different skies for awhile longer."

"I see. Well, it was nice sharing a night of inner exploration with you. Good-bye."

"I would not say that yet. Just because I do not wish to date you, it does not mean we will not meet again. I have a strong feeling you and I will see each other, though the reunion will be unplanned, as, ah . . . things develop."

"What does that mean?" he asked.

"I wish I had a little more of an idea but I do not. Take care."

She opened the door, waved and was gone.

CHAPTER ELEVEN

After eight long hours at the Crazy Horse Golf Course, four of them spent in 90+-degree heat, Lee and Frank agreed they'd go out together to wet their whistles. They'd been to the Golden Palace, Tumbleweed Tavern and Lucky Seven Lounge. Frank dabbled in nickel slots as Lee watched and sipped beer while bending Frank's ear about last week's experience with Soaring Eagle. Frank wasn't keen on the magical-mushrooms-road to cosmic insight. Though he liked his beer and occasional Jim Beam and thought the Marlboro Man was a great role model, his views on mood-altering substances took a big turn at peyote. Still, he seemed fascinated, though he wouldn't admit it, about the sensations Lee'd experienced and the two explanations, one scientific, the other occult, for the peyote's effects. It was like a married man listening to his single friend's graphic description of a one-night stand. Though he wouldn't let himself do what his friend was describing, the prospect was alluring.

After the Lucky Seven Lounge, Frank suggested they return to the Clear Sky Saloon for another game of pool. Lee agreed, saying he hoped their fellow pool players were less disposed to violence than the last time they'd been there. It being Friday night, the restaurant, casino and bar were all busier than usual, though the smaller and less fancy of the two bars, where the pool tables were, wasn't that packed. Folks were more interested in fancy meals, expensive drinks, bright lights and big jackpot possibilities of the casino than they were in hanging around a dimly lit little bar with a few pool tables and dart boards to while away the time. There was one unexpected bonus to playing pool here, Lee discovered, as they stepped into the place. The town's, and for that matter, the state's only bonafide, national star of big and little screens, and owner of this consortium of entertainment businesses, none other than Ricky Mann, stood behind the bar.

"Well I'll be dipped in horseshit if it ain't ole Ricky Mann hisself right over thar," Frank drawled with dripping sarcasm, his normal accent accented nearly beyond recognition. Lee chuckled. Flashbacks of watching "The Beverly Hillbillies" danced briefly through his head. Jed Clampett could rustle up a twang jest like ole Franky here and Jethro wasn't no slouch neither. *Hot damn, we got us a trio of drawlers now*, Lee mused.

"I've seen a few of his movies. Actually I think "Horse Droppings" was the best one and that was the parody of almost all his previous serious attempts. "The Journey Into the Endless Night" was a good book but their translation onto the silver screen fell as flat as a doughnut under a horse's hoof."

Frank narrowed his eyes at the failed simile but wouldn't dignify it with a verbal comment. Lee shrugged it off.

"So anyway, what's old Ricky doing back here on the Dakota prairie?" began Lee. "I thought he was shooting another movie in Hollywood."

"He is but lately he's been flying back here on weekends to check up on this place and work on the new project he's tryin' to get financed," Frank said as they approached the bar, a tiny mob of anxious celebrity-mongers lined up to talk with and get autographs from the local legend.

"The usual?" Lee asked as he stepped forward to wave down a bartender. Frank nodded.

A guy in his early twenties hustled toward the bill-waving patron.

"Yes sir?" he said, eyebrows raised, ear cocked.

"Pete and Dave's SPB and a Grain Belt."

"Bottle or tap on the Grain Belt?" he asked.

"Bottle please."

"Comin' right up."

Thirty seconds later, the bottles touched down on the counter in front of him. Lee gave a ten to the bartender, then handed Frank the Grain Belt while the barman got Lee's change. Ten seconds later, they were angling toward the trio of pool tables in the rear. A glance at Ricky revealed the mob's numbers had shrunk but five people remained, their expressions rapt with their closeness to such a bright star. The two nearest tables were taken but one closest to the rear wall was just waiting for a couple good old boys to play on. Lee found a suitable stick right off. It was slightly warped but close enough for his standards. Frank however, was a different story. Wedding rings had been chosen in less time than it took Frank to find a suitable pool cue. Lee almost asked him why he just didn't buy a pool cue so he wouldn't have to go through every time but Lee knew the answer. Frank was too damn cheap. He'd rather go through this every time he played than shell out thirty-five or forty bucks, at least, for a new one. Finally they were ready to begin. They were about three-quarters of the way through the game when Lee espied Ricky and another man coming their way. Lee didn't recognize the second guy. He was older, between forty and forty-five. A receding hairline, steel rim glasses and serious expression endowed the stranger with an intelligent, businessman-like aura. Three fans were almost at their heels but the man turned and said something to them. They glared at him for a few seconds before slowly turning around and walking away.

Lee turned to see how his opponent was faring. Frank had sunk two more balls while his attention had been away. Frank had only one ball left before the eight ball.

"Hey, knock that shit off," he said loudly.

Frank just smiled and lined up the next shot. Ricky Mann and the stranger skirted the far side of the right-hand table before circling around to their table.

"Howdy," said Ricky. "Say, how'd you boys like to play a game of doubles?"

"Fine with me," Lee said. He turned to Frank. "What do you think?"

Frank shrugged, then said, "Okay by me. Right after we're through we're with this game."

Ricky nodded and then produced a pack of cigarettes. He coaxed one out of the pack, slid in between his lips and flicked it alit. He pointed the holder of death sticks at his friend but the man shook his head emphatically. Meanwhile back at the pool table, Frank had pocketed the last solid. The problem was he'd left the cue ball on the opposite end of the table from the eight ball. Not only that, the black ball was plastered to the rail, approximately halfway between the two corner pockets. The only saving grace was that Lee's three remaining stripes were congregated around the right-hand side pocket. The path to the eight ball, though long, was clear. It reminded Lee of a long approach shot on the golf course. You'd normally like to be closer to the hole but if there was a monster bunker or huge water hazard in front of the green, you'd gladly settle for being seventy-five or a hundred yards farther away if you could make the water or sand disappear.

Frank made a vague motion with his head while somberly declaring, "Up in that corner."

Lee knew he which pocket he meant. He was trying to bank the eight back in the left-hand corner pocket. Frank brought the cue stick back and set the white ball in motion across the green field of felt. White met black for an instant, the cue ball pushing the eight off the rail and sending it on its merry way in the opposite direction. The spin imparted by Frank caused the cue ball to screech to a halt after rebounding off the rail. That left the white ball free to watch along with everyone else the results of its handiwork. Right from the onset it was obvious to Lee it was going to be close. Two feet from its target, Lee saw the black ball was headed toward the side rail. If it caught enough of the side rail, it'd bounce off and just barely miss dropping in. But if it merely grazed the side rail, it'd kiss off the tip of the pocket and fall in.

Of course, Lee hadn't thought what would happen if the eight ball hit right between the two options he'd mentally outlined. But it did. The black ball plunked off the side rail just before the pocket, ricocheted over and kissed of the tip of one pocket, then whizzed over and hit the other tip. The last tip imparted a slight spin onto the ball so that it not only rolled across from the rail but also just slightly sideways. The eight paused on the precipice, frozen in motion for a heartbeat like a high-wire trapeze artist in transition from one ladder to another.

Then it dropped out of sight.

"Well, pour vinegar and salt over my hemorrhoids. That son of a bitch went in," Lee drawled while shaking his head in mock disbelief.

"Nice shot, Franky. That was good."

"Franky?" he friend said, the emphasis clearly on the 'y'.

"Sorry, *Frank*," Lee corrected.

"Nice shot," Ricky said between drags on the cigarette. "How about a game of nine ball?"

Lee paused, threw a look at Frank. He looked thoughtful while chalking up his cue but said nothing.

"You boys know how to play nine ball?" Ricky asked while approaching the table with quarters in hand.

"Oh yeah," began Frank, "we're well acquainted with the game, isn't that right old buddy?" he said, his weathered face aimed in Lee's direction.

Thinking this was some kind of gamesmanship in which his friend was trying to make the opponents think Frank and he were better at the game than they truly were, thus giving them a psychological edge, he spat out, "Oh yeah."

Lee was familiar with the game, though he hadn't played for three or four years. The rules were simple enough. You played with nine balls and you had to shoot the balls in order. Since combinations were legal, it was perfectly legal for a player to use the object ball to make another ball. The main thing was that the first ball hit by the cue ball had to be one higher than the last ball. For example, if a player had shot in the one, two, three and four balls, he could choose to hit the five-ball into the eight and make the eight-ball in a pocket. That player would continue shooting. The next ball to be played would be the five-ball. In fact, he could even use the five-ball to make the nine to win the game. In that case, he would have to call the shot on the nine-ball to win the game. All other combinations did not have to be called.

"Yeah, I was just thinkin' whether we wanted to sink to that kind of game," said Frank.

"What the hell you talkin' about?" Ricky shot back as he pushed in the slot with the quarters in them. The balls were released from their prison and began their roll of freedom down toward where Ricky waited.

"I mean eight ball requires more skill and consistency. There ain't none of this early bird sinking of the winning shot."

"Well looky here, Jim. I'd say we got us a billiards elitist," said the actor, a smirk on his face.

"No, I just know how the different games really work and have played enough of them to know which ones I like better than others," Frank replied.

"So you wanna play nine ball or not?" demanded Ricky as he reached for the balls.

"Oh all right. Since this ain't no big ass tournament anyway, I reckon it doesn't much matter how much skill and how much luck is involved in the game."

Ricky Mann snorted a laugh and then racked the balls. After he'd finished, the handsome, blonde, Dying Tree native shoved the rack back into its slot and straightened up to his full height.

"This here is my agent and sometimes financial advisor, Jim Morton," Ricky said. After brief but polite "howdies" all around, the actor added, "and of course, I'm sure y'all know who I am."

Frank and Lee nodded their replies but didn't say anything. With the Ricky Mann shit all over the walls, one'd have to be daft or really, really drunk not see the resemblance between the man standing here and the surrounding photographs and posters. Verbal confirmation seemed redundant.

"I'm Lee Wyatt. This is Frank Leeds."

"Break 'em up," Ricky said while motioning at the triangular collection of ivory.

Frank looked at Lee but he shook his head.

"It's all yours, partner."

That was all the encouragement Frank needed. He bent over, eyed the shot while easing the cue stick back and forth across the V formed by thumb and index finger, and then blasted the cue ball. A white blur blew over the greenery and exploded into the rack. A second explosion followed the first as a rainbow of colors traced out nine different patterns of movement. Only the nine-ball, nestled snugly in the eye of the hurricane, failed to move less than six inches from its starting point. The three dropped out of sight while the one came to a rest right in front of the side pocket.

"You boys from round here?" Ricky asked.

"He's a native, I just got into town a couple weeks ago," Lee answered.

"Oh yeah, he does look familiar. Must have seen him in here a time or two, maybe in the gaming area too," Ricky said. Lee watched him draw in more nicotine, hold it for two seconds, then expel it toward the ceiling. The actor's eyes seemed in perpetual motion, his gaze never settling in one place for more than a few seconds. The thumb of his right hand tapped an incessant beat on the cue stick he held upright while waiting for his turn.

Frank had sunk the one ball. The two was next on his hit list. Though he had a clear shot at hitting the cue ball into it, three balls surrounded the two-ball like Indians around the good general at Custard's Last Stand. Frank cursed softly, straightened up, and chalked up while contemplating strategy.

"Any ideas?" he asked Lee.

"I think you should have left yourself better on the two," he said smiling.

Frank fixed him with a glare that would have scared the skin off a rattler.

"Didn't ask for ideas on to avoid the situation I'm in. I want ideas on how to deal with the cards I got in my hand."

"I know, I know," he replied.

Lee snuck a drink from the SPB and proceeded to survey the table. In the interim, Ricky had apparently grown weary of waiting for his turn. He was at the bar ordering some kind of drink. Lee pulled his concentration back to the pool game. His partner slowly approached the table.

"What if you hit the two into the seven-ball?" Lee said.

Frank paused, then said, "You mean in the far corner?"

"Yeah."

He nodded his head before saying, "I like that idea."

He turned to Jim Morton.

"You hear that? Two to the seven ball."

"Don't need to call combinations except for the nine ball," he said flatly.

"Oh hell, that's right. How could I forget that? Anyway, never mind. I'm just gonna shoot."

Which he did. And made the shot just as Ricky Mann returned with a tumbler of clear liquid over ice. Lee was betting on a vodka straight up. The actor grimaced like he was getting a cavity filled without Novocain when the seven plunked into the pocket. Setting the glass on the round table, Ricky traded nicotine for alcohol. While his cigarette warmed up, Frank's pool stick was already hot. He proceeded to sink the two, three and four balls. A five-eight combination narrowly missed going into a side pocket.

"Nice try, son. This table, as you'll soon discover for yourself, has an ever so slight lean to the left. Well, it's to the left if you're shootin' from down here, to the right if you're shooting' from down there," said Ricky.

"So it tilts toward the west," Frank said.

"Uh, yeah, that's right," Ricky replied hastily. "Well sir, let's see what the home team can do."

He stepped up the table after one last drag from the Marlboro. A little chalking and cursory perusal of the balls was all the preparation he needed. Ricky knocked the five, six and seven balls into three different pockets. A bank on the eight missed the shooter's target by a good six inches.

"Son of a bitch."

Ricky stalked away from the table. The actor cradled the drink like it was the Holy Grail as he murmured something to his agent. Meanwhile Lee plotted his shot. The eight had rolled to a stop right in the middle of the green surface. Like a straight uphill putt, Lee's shot, though not an easy one, wasn't especially tricky. If he hit it reasonably solid, it'd go in the far right-hand corner pocket. Without contemplating too much, he stepped up and smacked it. The black ball fell right in the middle of the pocket. The cue ball came to a halt right behind the nine.

"Good leave, partner," said Frank.

"Thanks," he said while chalking up the cue.

"I understand you're thinkin' about buildin' a casino and golf course out west of town," said Frank as he sat down at their little round table next to the pool table.

"That's right," the agent replied. "We're still working out the details."

"Sounds like the city of Dying Tree has been bendin' over backwards to help you finance this deal," Frank said while Lee finished chalking up.

"Yeah, they been real understanding so far," said Ricky.

"You know, it's been my experience that if a man bends over backwards long enough and often enough, he's liable to hurt himself."

Lee chuckled as he lined up the potentially game-winning shot. Ricky and his agent weren't laughing.

"What exactly are you sayin', son?"

Frank sipped his beer, and then slid a cigarette of his own out. While going through the lighting ritual, he said, "Only that some of the folks working for the town of Dying Tree might be a little too star struck to think clearly on this issue."

"Is that a fact?" Ricky said, hands on hips now, the drink momentarily forgotten, or maybe just unnecessary for now.

"Yes sir, I do believe it is," Frank said.

"The good folks of Dying Tree are just grateful and proud of their native son here," began Jim Morton, "and they want to honor him and boost the local and regional economies by extending a helping hand to Ricky. It's a marriage of private and public funds for the good of everyone involved."

Lee found it increasingly difficult to concentrate on pool. He shot a glance at his friend. He'd settled into his bar stool, soaking in the smell of the beer, soothing smoke of his cigarette and tension he'd conjured up with the challenges to their pool-playing opponents' business schemes.

"I sure the hell hope it's a long, fruitful marriage," Frank said simply before falling silent.

Lee knew there was a thundering herd of additional thoughts and opinions ready to stampede out of Frank's mind. His friend was diligent in locking the gate, however, as he apparently decided loosing them now would serve no purpose other than inflaming Ricky. The really important battles wouldn't be fought here in the Clear Sky Saloon. Not now.

Ricky dropped the aggressive stance, though his eyes were still huge and jittery. He sat back down, his agent doing likewise. Lee breathed a sigh of relief. He returned his focus to the game at hand. Despite its nearness to the nine-ball—it was only a foot away—the shooting angle toward any one pocket was poor. The best shot was a cut in the far left corner pocket. Lee announced his intention, took two practice strokes, and brought the cue stick forward. The gold and white ball rolled toward the target area. Right after he hit it, Lee was almost positive of a positive result. He hit right toward the middle of the pocket. Halfway there, Lee's confidence took a serious hit. Though the path of the nine had begun exactly as it ought, it was now veering slightly right of its original line. Lee'd not remembered Ricky's comment, or perhaps not believed it was true, about the table being slightly warped, thus causing slowly hit balls to curve right or left, depending which direction the ball was traveling. The break wasn't dramatic but it was there.

"Hang in there," Frank urged the ball.

A foot from the pocket, the ball seemed to straighten out. The problem was the table's lean had thrown the ball enough to the right to cause doubt about the success of the shot.

"I told ya about the table," Ricky Mann sang out while jumping to his feet.

The ball eased forward, caressed the right-hand tip of the pocket, spun back left, hovered halfway over the edge, then found one last eighth of a rotation. It dropped over the edge.

"Shit," muttered Ricky.

"Hell of a shot, pardner," Frank said.

"There was never a doubt, right?" Lee quipped while going for the chalk.

"We'll give you boys that one but next game'll be different," declared the actor while stomping toward the quarters on the side rail.

He threw the quarters in, shoved the silver slot forward and met the balls as they emptied at the far end of the table. He quickly lined the balls up inside the rack. The instant the rack was taken away, Lee blasted the cue ball. The white ball banged off the right-center part of the one ball, just as Lee'd planned. Though there was a flurry of activity as all nine balls in the rack scattered as if a grenade had been dropped in their midst, none went in.

"Fuck," Lee said softly. The word was normally too harsh for his tastes but a sudden realization he'd never win the South Dakota Man of the Year loosened his tongue. "Son of a fucking bitch, I can't believed nothing dropped."

Frank shook his head slowly.

"Don't worry. With breaks that good, you just needed a little break from the big guy and two or three balls will fall. But some nights I think the big guy's lookin' the other way. But if you keep swearin' like that, he'll start lookin' this way and let me tell yah, any good luck to be had won't be had by us."

Lee laughed softly. He was about to poke fun at his friend, chiding him about his previously hidden religious leanings when the night in the graveyard with Soaring Eagle roared into his mind. He remembered what Soaring Eagle said about the misplaced emphasis by most recreational mushroom users. They were so wrapped up with the sensations of the drugs that they failed to appreciate the significance of what they had, for a limited time, been shown. The veil had been lifted. He'd seen in a more dramatic way than he ever had the sheer fluidity of the world. Everything from atoms to thoughts to love flowed. The only thing that could stop the magical, mystical flow of Life was a closed mind. If Frank believed swearing would bring bad fortune to their pool-playing efforts because God objected to profanity, then who was to say he was wrong?

"Sorry Frank. I'll watch my mouth from now on," he said before plopping himself down in front of his beer.

Ricky Mann eyed the table with a crazed smile. He looked like a lioness that had just discovered a herd of sleeping wildebeests. The balls, disbursed so nicely and all fairly close to a pocket, laid like sleeping wildebeests, easy targets for the proficient, hungry predator. Ricky banged in the one, two, three, four and five balls without breathing, it seemed, but his leave for the six-ball wasn't optimally executed. Ricky left himself with a long cut shot that was far from a given. The actor took a few drags from the cigarette, and then finished his drink. Thusly fortified, he leaned over the table, took aim and launched the cue ball toward its distant target. It rattled off both points of the corner pockets before disappearing into the hole.

"Nice shot, Ricky," said Frank.

"Thanks," muttered Ricky without looking in Frank's direction.

The shooter was already moving toward the cue ball to line up the shot on the seven. He proceeded to fire in the last three balls with relative ease.

"Good game," Lee said right after the nine fell in the side pocket. "Well, should we play the tiebreaker?"

"No thanks. Gotta run," Ricky blurted out. He tossed his cue stick on the pool table and strode toward his agent. He nodded toward them and said, "Good playin' with ya. Maybe we'll play a game or two in my new place after it opens up."

They said nothing. Ricky and his agent wound their way through the crowd, several bar patrons smiling and saying something to Ricky as he passed by. The actor never stopped walking. He managed a nod or brief greeting but nothing more. One of the bartenders yelled something at him but Lee couldn't hear over the din. Ricky waved, spun around and left the bar. Jim Morton stayed behind, a sad, resigned expression settling over his face as he watched his client leave. Finally he went to the bar and ordered another drink.

"Left in an awful hurry," said Frank, his own cigarette on its last legs.

He rubbed its burning face into the ashtray until it was put out of its misery.

"Yeah, he sure did," Lee conceded. "I think he was on some kind of speed. In fact, I'm almost sure of it. Did you see his eyes bulging and the way he couldn't stand still for a second?"

His friend nodded.

"Yep, old Ricky Mann is flyin' high right now. Little-old-country-boy-turned-motion-picture-star. He seems to have the hometown folks right in the palm of his hand, don't he?" Frank said.

"Yeah, most of them anyway. I guess the key is how many of the town council people are in the palm of his hand," Lee said. "If he convinces enough of them that he's got a surefire money-maker of an idea, they'll subsidize most of the cost of the casino."

A shiver crawled up Lee's back. He shuddered. Was the air-conditioning that high? No, that wasn't it. Lee closed his eyes for five seconds. It was long enough to glimpse in his mind's eye an image whose source was unknown. The core image was fairly clear, though it turned fuzzy and indistinct as one moved away from the image's center. Lee saw a cloaked figure striding over a bridge. Under the stone structure flowed a river, not of water, but fire. The cloaked figure paused to peer at the spectacle below. So enticing was the intricate pattern in the lava flow that the figure leaned over even more, his feet now off the ground as he managed to balance precariously on the bridge's railing. The balancing act was short-lived. In his attempt to get an even closer look at the fiery flow, the figure toppled off the bridge and fell screaming into the river of flame.

"You okay?"

Lee's eyes popped open.

"Uh, yeah, sure, I'm fine," he said quickly.

"You sure?"

"Yeah. I was just thinking of something, that's all."

"You want to play one more game?" he asked.

"Yeah, but I need more alcohol," Lee said, his heart still beating a little faster than he'd like. "Tell you what, I'll go grab us a coupla beers if you want to rack 'em up."

"You got yourself a deal," replied Frank.

On Lee's trip to the bar, the customers didn't seem as innocent and simple as they had a minute ago. Maybe it was the trail of seething, dangerous psychic energy left by Ricky Mann's presence. Whatever it was, it set him on edge. Instead of being in tune with the invisible realms, Lee felt threatened by them. That was the problem with being too well connected, like the Web. A global village with everyone connected wasn't always so grand. If the person you were connected with had only their own selfish interests at heart, being intimately associated with them was dangerous. Their goals were certain to be different than yours. If you got in the way or could be used to their advantage, turning your back on them at the wrong time could have disastrous results. Lee sensed Ricky Mann's interests didn't involve the common good. What interested Ricky was Ricky and the public's perception of himself. Lee theorized that the cameras Ricky stood in front of while on the set were extended to his personal life. The mental camera of the actor's grossly overweight ego replaced the physical camera.

Lee ordered another SPB and Grain Belt Premium. He slapped a five in the bartender's hand and told him to keep the change. The grateful employee saluted him and said thanks.

On the way back to the pool table, he took great care to avoid bumping or even passing with a few inches of other saloon patrons. Ever since the vision of the cloaked figure—Ricky Mann, he postulated—walking through the underworld and eventually falling into the river of fire, a creeping, building paranoia dominated his mood. He thought he could sense auras around most people he passed by. The problem was he wasn't adept enough to interpret what he sensed. It was like a variation of the one line from The Wizard of Oz: "Are you a good aura or a bad aura?"

Once back at the pool table, Lee told himself this was going to be the last game. All the damn auras and psychic energy from everyone were buzzing around in his head. He felt too crowded by all the stuff going on at different levels of reality.

That damn Soaring Eagle, thought Lee, she started all this shit. Then he realized with blinding insight what the concept of a truly universal mind and the flowing nature of ultimate reality implied: LEE, AND EVERY OTHER HUMAN AS WELL, COULD BE VIRTUALLY ANYTHING OR ANYONE THEY WANTED. THE ONLY LIMITS WERE SELF-IMPOSED. That meant Lee was capable of bonding with every situation, of accepting the untarnished, unmitigated truth of his life at any given point in time. If the ego, a constructed, fabricated notion, was taken out of the picture, there was never any need for fear. Nothing threatened the individual with no ego because there was no fixed self to protect. There was such incredible freedom there if only he could see the truth of the way the universe really operated.

Finally he was able to just stop thinking about all the intricate, subtle, mostly imperceptible currents of energy and pathways to other worlds swirling and flowing all around and through him. Instead of trying to figure out the implications of what all that wild and exotic energy meant for him, Lee allowed the world around him do whatever it was going to do. However bizarre it all was, he knew intuitively that none of it was threatening. Not right now, anyway. At some future point, the seething energy and malevolent intentions of other realms might combine with people and forces in this world to create a threat that would have to be dealt with. For now, it was basically benign.

Lee smiled as Frank's break pocketed two balls and left him a clear shot on the one. He imagined how his friend must feel right now. Instead of resenting Frank and hoping he'd miss the next shot, Lee found himself honestly hoping his friend would make the next shot. After all, the sooner the game was done, the sooner they'd be out of this spirit-strewn, supernatural storehouse.

"Nice break, buddy," he said.

"Thanks."

Frank lined up the next shot.

CHAPTER TWELEVE

It'd been a short day at the golf course. Frank and he had worked so hard the first few weeks of Lee's employment that they were caught up. Whatever needed doing for the rest of the day, Frank could handle. With no work on his plate, Lee's initial buoyancy turned to trepidation for an instant before he caught himself.

FLOWING. F—L—O—W—I—N—G. He had to flow with each moment of each day. Assuming certain things were going to happen at certain times was not a good idea. A rigid, habit-loving mind was a mind out of touch with reality. Now that he wouldn't be working at the course, he was free to do whatever he needed or wanted to do. He decided a bike ride through town, or maybe in the countryside, would be just the thing to allow adequate time and space to reflect on the next course of action. Lee used his master key to enter the large equipment shed nearest the clubhouse. Near the front doors and to his right was his bicycle. The maroon Bianchi leaned sleepily against the wooden, cobweb-caked wall. He walked the bike through the front doors. After propping it up against the wall immediately left of the main doors, Lee locked up the shed.

After hopping on, he aimed the bicycle toward the highway at the end of the drive. When he reached the highway, he glanced right but then turned left. Heading back toward town for some reason seemed preferable to the countryside. While it was true the countryside would give him more time for quiet contemplation, Lee wanted to be around more people. While he enjoyed working at the golf course, there weren't many opportunities for socialization. Besides talking to Eileen Eide—the owner—and Frank, most of his exposure to other human beings was from a distance. He saw dots or vague shapes putting or driving from at least two to three hundred yards away. A trip through town would bring him closer to people, even though he might not sit down and have a heart-to-heart talk with any of them, the mere proximity to other human beings was a soothing, comforting prospect. For several minutes, he stopped thinking of anything except negotiating the road, which was easy enough because of the straightness of the route. As he neared Dying Tree's downtown, his mind began growing restless. It was like a small child tugging on her mother's dress or father's pants leg. If the parent were busy conversing with another adult, the tugging from below could be ignored for awhile. After so long the parent gives in and sees what the little tyke wants. Curiosity and some irritation cause them to give audience to the interloper.

Such was the case now. In this instance, what the mind wanted to make him notice was not at all clear. It was a nagging feeling that Lee had failed to take care of some aspect of his life. There was something about his old life, the pre-prairie period, that he'd failed to adequately attend to. Instead of ticking off a laundry list of possibilities, Lee just kept pedaling and intentionally pointed his concentration in the opposite direction.

Several minutes later, after he'd temporarily forgotten about the problem, the answer hit him as solidly as a horseshoe to the back of the head: he hadn't truly broke the off the relationship with his wife Mary. He'd left the Post-It Note saying something about working out the details of the divorce later and that he was leaving her (I AM OUTTA HERE, as Dennis Miller used to say on Saturday Night Live) but that was all he said. Maybe that was enough for Mary but it wasn't enough for him. He had to make more of an explanation than that, if not for Mary's sake then for his own peace of mind. He'd left too many things hanging.

But how should he communicate with Mary? Sure, he could call her up but then she'd interrupt him while he was explaining himself. Or maybe she'd just not really pay attention to what he was saying. No, a phone call didn't sound like the best way. After braking and slowing at a stop sign, Lee pedaled quickly through after seeing no cross traffic approaching. A block ahead, he saw a sign: DYING TREE PUBLIC LIBRARY.

Lee smiled. Nowadays, where there were libraries, there were computers. And where there were computers, there was e-mail. He could send her a long, carefully thought out letter explaining why he'd left and what to expect from him and how they should proceed from this point on. The prospect of attending to this final clean-up task from the transitional period of his life instilled added vigor in his legs and lungs. He sped across the pavement of the street until pulling even with the library. Lee veered hard right, then braked hard enough to squeal the tires. He walked the bike to the bicycle rack fifty yards to the right of the main entrance to the library. The combination to the bike lock was easily enough recalled by a man with his accounting background. Figures seemed to find a nice cozy place to hang out in his mind until they were needed at the surface. Then they swam effortlessly across through the bare minimum of mental waterways until reaching the surface of his consciousness where they were needed.

Lee strode through the revolving door and into the lobby. He glanced left and saw computer monitors arranged in a row along a wall not more than a hundred yards from him. He headed right for them, easily winding his way through the groups of fellow library patrons and staff. There were two open computers right in the middle. He sat down at the one on the left. He had to dig out his address book to see what the user name and password were for his universal e-mail account were. After accessing it, he addressed the electronic correspondence to his wife's work computer (they had no Internet access at home).

At first he could only stare at the screen while his fingers covered the keys of the home row or whatever in the hell it was called on a computer keyboard. Then like a Ouija board working its magic, thoughts and feelings were channeled through his fingertips and onto the screen:

DEAR MARY,

HI—IT'S LEE. I KNOW MY DEPARTURE WAS DONE SUDDENLY AND ALL BUT GIVEN THE CIRCUMUSTANCES AND MY FEELINGS AT THE TIME, IT FELT RIGHT TO DO IT THAT WAY. I'M SURE THERE ARE A THOUSAND DETAILS AND LEGAL THINGS WE'LL HAVE WORK OUT. I'LL HAVE TO CONSULT A LOCAL LAWYER OR SEARCH THE INTERNET FOR LEGAL ADVICE OR SOMETHING. ANYWAY, I WANTED TO SAY SOME THINGS THAT NEED TO BE SAID.

NUMBER ONE, I STILL LOVE YOU BUT NOT IN THE WAY YOU MIGHT THINK. I LOVE YOU LIKE I LOVE A GOOD FRIEND. I KNOW WE STARTED OFF OUR RELATIONSHIP ELEVEN YEARS AGO AS LOVERS AND AS I REMEMBER IT, WE HAD OUR SHARE OF PASSIONATE, GREAT SEX. THOSE TIMES ON THE GOLF COURSE AT NIGHT WERE ESPECIALLY MEMORABLE,

MOSTLY BECAUSE OF THAT ONE REMARK YOU MADE ABOUT YOUR MOM ASKING YOU THE NEXT MORNING HOW YOU GOT GRASS STAINS ON YOUR KNEES. BUT ANYWAY, OVER THE YEARS, AS YOU OBVIOUSLY KNOW, THE PHYSICAL PART OF OUR RELATIONSHIP VIRTUALLY DISAPPEARED. THAT WAS THE RESULT OF A DEEPER DIVISION, A CHASM BETWEEN OUR SOULS, I WOULD SAY. WE DIDN'T DISLIKE EACH OTHER BUT WE WEREN'T AS ATTRACTED TO EACH OTHER AS WE FIRST WERE.

THE OBVIOUS QUESTION IS WHY. I THINK IT WAS A LACK OF COMMON INTERESTS. OPPOSITES MAY ATTRACT BUT RARELY DO THEY STAY TOGETHER. YOU'VE GOT TO HAVE ENOUGH AREAS OF INTEREST TO SHARE WITH EACH OTHER TO KEEP THE SACRED BOND INTACT. IT SEEMS TO ME THE ONLY THING WE BOTH CARED ABOUT WAS DRINKING OURSELVES INTO A STUPOR EVERY SIX OR SEVEN DAYS. THAT WAS CERTAINLY A SHARED RITUAL BUT BEYOND THAT, THERE WASN'T MUCH.

I'VE KNOWN FOR SEVERAL MONTHS ABOUT YOUR BOYFRIEND. OR IS IT PLURAL? NO, I'M PRETTY SURE IT'S JUST ONE. AT ANY RATE, I ADMIT I WAS UPSET WHEN I FIRST ADMITTED TO MYSELF WHAT WAS REALLY GOING ON. BUT NOW, I'M OVER IT. THE FACT THAT I DIDN'T CONFRONT YOU ABOUT IT SHOWS THAT I JUST DIDN'T CARE ENOUGH TO FACE THE SITUATION HEAD-ON. IT'S LIKE I SAID BEFORE ABOUT OUR DYING SEX LIFE. THE LACK OF PASSION ISN'T SOMETHING THAT CAN BE ISOLATED FROM EVERYTHING ELSE. YOU HAVE TO START AT THE DEEPEST, MOST FUNDAMENTAL PART OF YOURSELF, WHICH IS WHAT I CALL THE SOUL. OUR SOULS HAD GROWN APART FIRST. EVERYTHING ELSE THAT HAPPENED WAS AN INEVITABLE CONSEQUENCE OF THAT SPLITTING APART. THE FACT THAT YOU ENDED UP WITH ANOTHER MAN AND THAT I DIDN'T CARE ENOUGH TO CONFRONT YOU ABOUT IT IS PERFECTLY UNDERSTANDABLE. IT WAS A NATURAL

PROGRESSION THAT FLOWED FROM THE BREAK-UP OF OUR SPIRITS.

I HONESTLY HOPE AND PRAY THINGS WORK OUT FOR YOU. IF YOU REALLY LOVE THIS OTHER MAN AND HE GENUINELY LOVES YOU, AND YOU BOTH FEEL MARRIAGE IS RIGHT FOR YOU, THEN I HOPE YOUR NEW UNION WORKS OUT. BUT PLEASE DON'T MAKE THE SAME MISTAKE WE DID. REALLY THINK ABOUT HOW YOU FEEL ABOUT HIM. DO YOU TRUST HIM? DOES HE TRUST YOU? AND DO YOU HAVE IMPORTANT THINGS THAT YOU BOTH CARE ABOUT?

IF SO, THEN YOU'RE PROBABLY READY TO GET MARRIED OR AT LEAST CO-HABITATE. BUT WHATEVER HAPPENS WITH THIS OTHER GUY, I WISH YOU NOTHING BUT GOOD LUCK AND HAPPINESS. FOR ME, I WAS WEARING THE HUSBAND COSTUME FOR ALL THOSE YEARS BUT I WASN'T REALLY FEELING THE PART LIKE A GOOD HUSBAND WOULD. I DON'T KNOW THAT I'LL BE PLAYING THAT PART AGAIN, AT LEAST NOT IN THE NEXT FEW YEARS.

WELL, I THINK THAT'S JUST ABOUT ALL FOR NOW. IF YOU NEED TO SEND ME ANYTHING LIKE LEGAL PAPERS TO SIGN OR WHATEVER, OR IF YOU NEED TO REACH ME, I'M STAYING IN A ROOM IN THE SECOND STORY OF THE CLUBHOUSE AT THE CRAZY HORSE GOLF CLUB IN DYING TREE, SOUTH DAKOTA. IF YOU HAPPEN TO SPEAK TO MY MOM BEFORE I DO, PLEASE GIVE HER THE ADDRESS. IF YOU WANT TO RESPOND TO THIS E-MAIL, FEEL FREE. I'M NOT SURE HOW OFTEN I'LL BE CHECKING IT AS I DON'T HAVE A COMPUTER WHERE I'M STAYING AND I'M SURE I WON'T BE MAKING DAILY TRIPS TO THE LIBRARY TO USE THEIR COMPUTERS. ANYWAY, I HOPE THINGS WORK OUT FOR YOU. NO HARD FEELINGS, HUH?

—LOVE LEE

Lee clicked the SEND button, waited for a confirmation from Yahoo that it was sent, and then after seeing the message, bent over, closed his eyes, and allowed his head to rest against the monitor. Several seconds, perhaps longer, passed before he opened his eyes and pushed away from the screen. He signed off the Internet, jumped to his feet, and strode out through the library toward his waiting bicycle. He hadn't felt so energized in a long, long time. Now he felt completely unencumbered. The one major act he hadn't attended to had now been taken care of. He felt free to become anything and anyone he needed to be. The template of his life was so broad and free flowing that it couldn't rightly be called a template at all. But there was a stabilizing force he was connected to and that was this: In the giant castle of life, there were a limitless number of doorways to the heavenly plane. For some, it was a particular religion such as Christianity or Hinduism. For others, it was doing good deeds, which could be sparked by the first one. For others, it was a particular drug. For others, it was sex or sports or food.

For himself, Lee decided right there and then, just as he'd begun going through the revolving door that would shoot him outside, that he would take whatever doorway that seemed best suited to his spiritual essence at the time. He would not rule out any option. He would do and become whatever and whomever he needed to be to make the universe a better place. If he could brush aside and see past all the earthly, worldly glitter and get right to the heart of the matter, he'd be fine. That meant not looking back to see how he would have handled it in the past nor fretting over the possible consequences if he failed. It meant simply perceiving the world and most importantly, himself, the way they truly were and then matching up the two to act wisely and compassionately. His goal was be so utterly in tune with the universe that if he made the people OUT THERE happier, that would make himself happier because there was no difference between OUT THERE and IN HERE (i.e.—his inner self).

Outside now, he bounced over to his bike, spun the numbers on the lock until he hit the correct combination and freed his two-wheeled, eighteen-geared friend from its bonds. He hopped on the mechanical beast and began the trip back to his home on the golf course. As he cruised down the street, he occasionally put himself in the shoes of people he passed by or imagined himself in the bodies of birds he saw perched on telephone wires or flying through the air. Once he even envisioned himself in the body of a worm crawling across the sidewalk in front of him. Then he saw imagined an incredibly complex, interconnected web of relationships between himself and all those living beings—human, animal, and otherwise—that he was right in the middle of. And not only was he in the middle of this web right now, he was in it every instant of every day of his life.

He slowed to let a stream of cars and trucks cross in front of him. Lee recognized the driver of the last car in the group. It was Clem Nelson, a regular at the Crazy Horse Golf Club. Clem smiled and threw him a wave, which Lee returned. He began moving faster, the turn-off for County Road 36 coming up in four blocks. Now Lee better appreciated what Soaring Eagle had said about peyote. The key was not the experience of the high itself. It was what the peyote showed, namely the basic, pure, unbroken unity of all things and beings on all planes. For the enlightened soul, the real excitement came not during the high but after it was all over.

As an American citizen, Lee'd been as free, in theory, as anyone on the planet. Now he saw how much he'd limited his own freedom over the last twenty-six years or so. Once he'd graduated from high school, his self-image was so rigidly set that he'd essentially constructed a jail cell around himself. He'd been moving around in these tiny circles within the prison cell all these years. He hadn't even thought to do many things simply because it would have meant stepping outside the neat little rectangle of his rigid, well-defined personality. Now that he'd seen how the universe really worked, thanks to Soaring Eagle, Lee felt freer than ever in his entire life. He'd no doubt been this free from the time he was a baby all the way through grade school. The problem was he hadn't appreciated it at the time. That was the paradox of freedom. When one truly experienced it, the individual rarely realized it. But now Lee both realized it and appreciated it. He rode faster than he'd ever ridden before. The trip home was infinitely shorter than the trip into town.

CHAPTER THIRTEEN

After returning to his home at the golf course, Lee showered for a good fifteen minutes. Halfway through the shower, he considered pushing the knob in so that the water came out of the faucet instead of the showerhead. A slow, luxurious bath was more in tune with what he wanted. However, once in the midst of the shower, Lee found the inertia of decision too powerful to overcome. The water flowed and flowed over his body, his legs especially feeling the effects of the bike ride. Once the watery barrage ended and he'd toweled himself off, Lee couldn't resist the pull of the bed. He crawled under the covers, pulled out a SPORTS ILLUSTRATED issue, and was asleep within five minutes. The magazine slipped from his hands after he nodded off.

Two hours later, Lee struggled to consciousness. He debated whether to plunge fully into the world of wakefulness or return to the realm of restful snoozing. Finally he decided that waking was better than sleeping right now. But if he was going to stay awake, he was going to do something that was not only fun but informative. He figured with Dying Tree's historical significance, there'd be ample cultural events to meet his criteria. Lee shuffled down the stairs leading to the clubhouse's main level. He recalled seeing the town newspaper lying around on various tables in the restaurant. It took four tables of searching to find but he met his goal. Thumbing through the Dakota Voice, he eventually found a section called LOCAL EVENTS. Under that heading was a book signing, country singer concert, regional golf tournament, and new exhibit at an art gallery. Lee was about to turn the page but he spotted one more event listed at the bottom of the page:

> FRONTIER BOB PLAY—daily shows at 5, 7, 9 and 11 p.m. at the Prairie Land Playhouse.

"Damn, that's the ticket," he muttered. Lee'd heard all about Frontier Bob from Frank on one occasion in a local saloon. The man was the town's legend, a man who'd grown much larger than life. It was too late for the five o'clock show but he could make the seven o'clock one.

Lee decided he'd call Frank to see if he'd wanted to go along. He wasn't harboring really high hopes. Even though Frank didn't strike him as an artsy-type, he'd lived in the town so long he'd probably seen the show at least once. Besides, Frank was a local. He'd no doubt heard the history behind Frontier Bob so many times he could probably recite the pertinent facts verbatim. But what the hell, maybe old Frank hadn't seen the drama in many a year. He punched in Frank's number. He picked up on the third ring.

"'Hello."

"Hey Frank. It's your old pool partner, Lee Wyatt."

"Yeah?"

"I was thinking about going to the Frontier Bob play that starts at seven tonight. I was wondering if you wanted to go with me."

Dead silence.

"Frank? You still there?"

"Yep. Just thinkin', that's all."

"Oh, I see. Well, you've no doubt already seen it and all—"

"Nope."

"You're kidding?" Lee exclaimed.

"Nope. Dead serious," Frank replied.

"How come?"

"How come I'm dead serious?"

"Very funny, Frank. No, how come you've never seen the play? I know you're not exactly an artsy type but even so, I'd have thought you would have seen at least one showing."

"When you live in the town, you hear and see so much advertisin' for the play and Frontier Bob in general that you kinda grow numb on the topic, know what I mean?"

Lee nodded, then remembered he was on the telephone. Frank couldn't see him nod.

"Yeah, I know exactly what you mean," he quickly added. "To you, Frontier Bob is like your toothbrush or an old flannel shirt you'd had for what seems like forever. Repeated exposure dulls the shine of the star. Your mind lapses into screen saver mode at the mention of his name."

"Screen saver? What the hell is that?" he asked.

"They're on computer screens. If you don't hit a key or use the mouse for a certain period of time, a picture or design appears on the screen. And there's always some kind of repetitive movement by the designs or letters or whatever. It's the same action over and over and over so that it's like your computer is daydreaming to kill time until you wake up and start doing something intelligent with it."

"Oh. Well, anyway, I'll go with yah. Might be interestin'. Probably learn something I never knew bout old Frontier Bob. Sides, it'll be a nice change from shootin' or hittin' the bars. Tell you what, I'll pick you up at twenty to seven."

"Great. See you then."

*　　*　　*

The early-evening air was cooling quickly. Eighty-five degree temperatures and shirt-sticking humidity quickly gave way to falling thermometers and a rogue wind. A block from the Prairie Land Playhouse, they noticed something strange was going on. People were walking away from the theater doors instead of walking through them. A half-block from the entrance, Lee saw a bright pink sign taped on the front door. A couple of people were reading what it said. One person shook their head before wheeling around and striding away. The other person did likewise a few seconds later. A person in an approaching group of three said something to him. He gave them an answer of some kind. Then they turned around and began walking across the street toward Kevin's Rib Heaven.

"Somethin' fishy is goin' on," Frank declared solemnly.

"It appears so," Lee replied.

A group of four folks had just finished reading the sign. They too were shaking their heads and frowning. Lee and Frank were close enough to read the black lettered message:

> FRONTIER BOB PERFORMANCES HAVE BEEN CANCELLED THROUGH NEXT SATURDAY. STANLEY MOSS, WHO NORMALLY PORTRAYS FRONTIER BOB, IS OUT OF TOWN ON VACATION. HIS UNDERSTUDY, TOMMY BLACK, IS ILL WITH A VIRAL INFECTION.

"Well shit on a shingle," Lee said. "That sucks."

"Don't it, though," Frank said. "Guess we're off to the saloons after all."

"I reckon," he replied, not even realizing how much like a seasoned cowboy he sounded.

Lee followed Frank. He trusted his friend's judgment so he didn't bother asking where they were going. Whichever bar he chose would be a fine selection. Frank led Lee into a place called The Never Ending Pouring. It was quaint place. Not too big, limited lighting, several holes in the carpeting, a haze of cigarette and cigar smoke hanging in the air like an accusation. While Frank ordered a couple of beers, Lee found a booth for them. He decided on the very back one. An electronic dartboard flashed its charms at him but he resisted the temptation. A newspaper laid open, its guts revealed. Lee settled into the seat. A glance at the bar told him Frank had just ordered and was waiting the bartender's return. His gaze dropped down to the newspaper's presentation of the latest goings-on.

The front page headline blared, "CRUCIAL TOWN COUNCIL VOTE NEXT MONDAY ON RICKY MANN PROJECT." He began reading the article underneath:

> Ricky Mann's quest to begin a major regional entertainment complex will depend on the outcome of the town council vote next Monday. Ricky Mann's agent, Jim Morton, says the star and his investment group, believed to be three or four businessmen from the West coast, will pay for only one-third of the proposed $225-million-dollar project. In addition, the Mann group is seeking a package of economic incentives. Among the incentives are real estate tax relief, donated land for the building site, free sewer and water line installation, and a donated liquor license. The city of Dying Tree, lugging around a $3,000,000-loan for construction of the new city hall and civic center, must decide whether they want to give away so much to a casino, saloon, and golf course that would face stiff competition from a market teeming with veteran, proven competitors. Supporters of the idea, including Ricky Mann himself, are banking on the star's sprawling following, especially among those between 18 and 35 years of age, to propel the business above the crowd.

"Find somethin' interesting?"

Lee looked up to discover his friend and two bottles of beer studying him.

"Yeah, matter a fact I did. Reading about our old buddy's entertainment complex deal. The big town-council vote is fast approaching."

Frank slid into the booth across from him. His friend slid the chili pepper beer across the table. Lee spread his fingers and thumb. The glass container, like a perfectly executed pass from Wayne Gretsky or Mario Lemieux, hit right in the middle of the target.

"So what do you think about the vote? Aye or nay?"

Frank threw a frown in his direction as he brought the Grain Belt to his lips.

"Sorry. I meant yes or no, thumbs up or thumbs down, pass or fail," said Lee.

After a sigh and five seconds of staring at the electronic dart board, Frank leaned toward him.

"I'll tell you what, that is an interestin' question. All right, we got seven town council members and one mayor. Ralph Tergis, the mayor, already said he'll accept whatever decision the council makes. Town ordinances give the mayor the power to veto decisions by the town council that are not unanimous. The council can debate the issue some more and then vote again. If it's not unanimous the second time, the proposal fails. But if Ralph is true to his word, which I expect he will be, there won't be any call for debatin' the issue. Whatever the council decides, Ralph'll go along with it."

"I see," Lee began, "how do you think the council will vote? Do you know who's all on the town council?"

"Let's see, you got Bob McCallum and Rosie Dale. They're the two ringleaders since they've been on the council longer'n anybody. Bob is dead set against it while old Rosie, I bet, will vote for it. She ain't sayin' nothin' to the reporters or made any official statements but I'd bet my last dime she'll vote yes.

"Then yah got Frank O'Connor. I see him at the gun club once in awhile. He's a good old boy, a fine Irishman with head of hair so bright he's like a damn lighthouse. He don't trust Ricky Mann worth a lick. There ain't no way in hell he'd vote for givin' away all those things to someone who's already richer than half the town put together."

"So we got two nos and one yes so far," Lee chimed in.

Frank continued without acknowledging the remark.

"Then yah got Mildred Foster. She told a friend of my ma's that she's probably going to vote no. Don't think Dying Tree needs another place to gamble and drink and hit a golf ball around. She and her husband are raisin' two little boys and I don't think she's crazy bout the town's main draw bein' booze and slot machines.

"Next is Ron Deere. He's got every damn video ever released that Ricky was in. Claims he's studied the numbers and all but I think he'll vote with yes no matter what the numbers really say."

"The nos are still ahead by one," said Lee.

"Yep, three to two for runnin' old Ricky's scheme right outta town. Problem there's two more folks to be heard from," Frank replied before sipping his beer. "The interestin' thing bout the last two is that whichever way each one votes, it'll be the same as the other one."

"Oh?" Lee said.

Two guys had just begun playing darts at the board near their booth. The one preparing to throw first wore a black tee shirt that announced in red letters, I'VE SEEN THE ANTI-CHRIST AND HE'S SITTING IN THE OVAL OFICE.

"Yep," Frank continued, "Agatha Hines and Steve McCall. Both lost long-time spouses in the last five years. I'm pretty sure they're just good friends, seein' as how they're both over eighty years old, but hell, who knows? They could end up marryin' next month. Anyways, they're real tight. They tend to see things the same way. Whichever way one goes, the other'll follow."

"And how do you think they'll vote?" asked Lee as he watched a dart whiz past their table.

"Most people say they'll vote no cause they're both are real good about attendin' church and helpin' charities and such, which they are."

Lee leaned forward and said, "But . . ."

Frank regarded his bottle of Grain Belt for a bit, then turned his attention squarely onto Lee.

"But I know somethin' most folks don't know bout Agatha," he began, pausing for effect. It worked as Lee edged his ass a few inches closer to the edge of his seat. "And that is she loves to gamble. Slot machines mostly, a game of blackjack here and there, but mostly nickel and dime slots."

"How do you know this?" Lee asked.

"One of the members at Crazy Horse Golf Club has an uncle who works at a casino in Good Earth, which is around fifty miles from Dying Tree. He's seen Mildred at his casino every Friday and Saturday night for the last four years."

"The last four years?" he asked, eyebrows reaching for the ceiling.

"Yep. She likes her slots, I reckon. Course maybe there's already enough gamblin' places round here, at least as far as she's concerned. But my hunch is that old Agatha would love to have another big casino, somewhere right close by where she could get lost in and not have any of the locals know she was there. It sounds like Ricky's place'd be a lot bigger than most places round here."

"And even if Mildred wasn't interested in going to Ricky's place, she'd still probably be in favor of it on general principles. It'd be like asking a football fan if they'd vote to have a football stadium built."

"That's right, partner."

Lee sat back, his back flush with the booth.

"Damn, if that's the case, then the deal's going to go through," he said.

"Sure looks like it," Frank replied.

"What are your thoughts about that prospect?" Lee asked.

Frank gazed long and hard at his beer, sat back in his chair, and then finally leaned forward again.

"I'd say it's like leadin' Satan to a seat in your church. Course I'm just a humble golf course maintenance worker."

"But that's how you feel?" Lee asked.

"Yep."

"How bad do you think it'll be?"

"Bad enough."

"What does that mean?" Lee asked above the growing din.

Since Lee'd first sat down, the number of customers in the place had doubled. All the booths and all but one barstool at the counter were occupied. There were still two tables open but at this rate, they'd be taken before long.

"If the town sinks all this money into a business that don't fly and then goes belly up itself, that means there won't be no more schools, library, street cleanin', snow plowin', park maintenance, and so on. If that happens, most of the residents'll pack up and move on down the road to another town. Some of 'em will only move down the road maybe twenty, thirty miles, but some of it will go a ways further. The result is all those businesses along Main Street will lose a helluva lot of customers."

"But aren't most of their customers tourists? They're obviously not from town," Lee said while absently running his thumb over the neck of the beer bottle. The guy with the oval office/Satan tee shirt was whooping up a bulls' eye he'd just thrown.

"Yeah, most of their money comes from tourists but there's a big enough chunk that comes from locals. Most casinos, bars and restaurants and such are okay but there's not a lot room to fall before they'd have real problems makin' a go of it. They need every dollar they can get. Take away the money the residents spend and most of them places wouldn't survive," said Frank.

"I see," Lee said.

He leaned back against the booth's back and poured down the rest of his beer. The chili pepper at the bottom of the bottle stared at him.

"But that's assuming a lot," Lee began, the wheels in his brain again turning. "That's assuming the project falls flat. It could be a thriving success, right?"

Frank took a cigarette out, lit it, sucked in a mouthful of carcinogenic smoke, and exhaled out his nostrils. He sighed before saying, "Suppose so."

Frank picked up the Grain Belt and swallowed the last few drops.

"But you don't think it will, do you?" Lee persisted.

"Nope."

"Why is that?"

"Just don't trust the guy. I mean if a man is so jazzed up on some kinda speed or whatever the hell you call it that he can't even finish a simple best of three pool series, how in the hell do you expect him to have a successful business?"

Lee had no reply for that. In way, it seemed like an arbitrary, simplistic method to evaluate a man's entrepreneurial skills. But now that Lee thought it over a bit more, he began to see the merit of the method. After all, success in any field ultimately depended on the individual's character. Knowledge and luck were major players but overriding both were character. If the person was wise enough to look at situations and do what was right for everyone concerned, that wisdom was worth more than a certain number of credits or certain number of years of experience in this field or that field.

"Yeah, I see your point," he finally said. Lee downed the rest of his beer.

"Ready to go?" Frank asked after another drag on his cigarette.

Lee nodded. They arose and headed for the door. En route, they debated which saloon to visit next. By the time they reached the door, they still hadn't made a decision. One thing was for certain. They wouldn't be going to the Clear Sky Saloon tonight. That place still scared Lee.

CHAPTER FOURTEEN

"You want us to do what?" asked Red Troester, owner of the Pioneer Construction Company.

As the most respected and reasonably priced construction company in the Dying Tree area, their bid was accepted by the Ricky Mann-led investment group. He was set to knock off for the day. Troester seriously considered letting the phone call go into voice mail. However, his long-standing practice of answering whatever call he could overrode his first inclination.

"I want all the construction equipment you're going to use for the entertainment complex on site and ready to go the night before the town council meeting. That way, after they approve the economic incentives package, y'all will be ready to roll. I want this project done as soon as possible. The sooner ya'll start, the sooner ya'll finish," declared Ricky Mann.

"With all due respect, Mr. Mann, it ain't that easy. I got my men and equipment allocated to different jobs. Our original agreement stated we were to begin work if and when the council approved the economics package. I got my personnel and equipment committed to other customers through the end of the day next Monday."

"Listen here, this job'll be the biggest thing you've done or will ever do in your life. Don't be givin' this line of shit about your men and equipment being committed elsewhere. If you want this job, then make sure you're ready to start pouring the foundation come next Tuesday morning."

Five seconds of silence, then, "All right, I'll have my guys there with all the equipment in place by next Tuesday morning if you guarantee payment to cover the cost of moving staff and equipment," said Red.

"What's that gonna run?"

"I'd say $30,000 will cover it."

"I'll talk to my financial people and make sure it's covered," replied Ricky Mann.

"All right. Just have your money guy call Mike Burns. He's our CFO," grumbled Red.

"No problem. I'll do that. You just make sure you're ready to go on Monday so after they vote yes on Monday night, you can go like a bat out of hell come Tuesday morning."

"What's your big rush? It'd only take another day if we waited until Tuesday to start hauling equipment to the site," Red said.

"That's a day too late. Time's a wastin'. This entertainment complex is just what the area needs," Ricky said, "and the sooner it's built, the sooner the fix'll be in place."

"Is that right?" Red replied somewhat dubiously.

"That's right, son. This town is starvin' for a big-time, big-name-backed place like this. I'm gonna plant some of the Hollywood magic right here in Dying Tree."

"Whatever you say, Mr. Mann. Me and my men will do our job. You just make sure we get paid on time."

"Yeah, yeah. Don't worry. You will," Ricky assured him. "Call me if there are any complications. Otherwise I'll see you and your crew at the site, all locked and loaded, come next Tuesday morning at the site."

*   *   *

They were halfway up the hillside, the gradient growing steeper as they climbed. Lee had to keep grabbing trunks of trees to keep from toppling over backwards and rolling back down the incline. Between ragged breaths, chuckles from Frank peppered the air. After fulfilling their duties at the golf course, Frank had initiated this foray through the woods. He told Lee there was a great place to practice shooting, a nice secluded area where Frank had set up targets.

"Are we getting close to this secret practice area?" Lee asked, his forehead splattered with sweat. "I'm not in extraordinarily good shape, you know. Golf is not exactly a physically taxing sport. Psychologically it's the worst, of course, but . . ." He paused to catch a breath, then, " . . . it's on an aerobic par with bowling or maybe curling."

"It's a little more strenuous than that, pardner," began Frank, his tobacco-tinged voice no longer quite as confident as normal.

His lungs strained to keep up with what his mind was trying to tell his mouth to say, the breathy quality and slower cadence of his speech stripping away some of Frank's facade of aloof self-sufficiency.

"Specially on a hilly course. Ya almost gotta be a damn billy goat to walk the new course they built just outside McCall Village."

The burst of speech left Frank gasping for breath. Studying the territory directly ahead, Lee thought he saw a spot thirty yards away and slightly above them where the ground leveled off. Deciding to give Frank's lungs a much-needed rest, he didn't ask if they were close to the plateau leading to or perhaps containing Frank's practice area. They'd find out soon enough if he were right about the terrain leveling off.

"We're here. No more climbin'. Yah happy now?" Frank said just after cresting the hill and stepping onto level land.

"Yes, darn it, I'm extremely happy," he replied after hoisting himself up and over the hill.

Staring back at him were bullet-riddled cardboard cutouts of five generic male figures. All were supported from the rear by boards running from the middle of the back on a diagonal line into the ground four feet behind the figures. Next to the quintet were a variety of configurations, all of them standing atop plywood platforms that were supported from the bottom on each of the four corners by trios of cement blocks. From left to right, there was a pyramid of bowling pins, line of eight Grain Belt bottles, scarecrow nailed to a cross, and an old chalkboard.

"Wow, you've got quite a set-up here, Frank old buddy. How in the hell did you haul all that stuff up here?"

"Hauled it up in the pickup. There's a road goin' up the other side of the hill," Frank answered.

"Shit, now you tell me!" Lee said.

"Every once in awhile, I get a hankerin' for a little physical exercise that's above and beyond golfin', you know? I thought a climb up the hillside would do us both good. Hell, you don't smoke. I figured if I could make it, you sure the hell could."

"Yeah, I suppose you're right," Lee conceded while mopping off his forehead with his right shirtsleeve. "But you're still a son of a bitch and don't ever forget that."

Frank arched an eyebrow.

"So what about guns? You didn't bring any along that I saw. Of course, if they were concealed handguns, I wouldn't have seen them," he said.

"Got 'em up here already," his friend said while walking toward a small wooden structure.

It had only one window. The shed was about five by five by seven feet. A padlock with combination lock kept everyone but the owner out. The glass window could be broken, Lee supposed, but the burglar would then be a criminal twice over. He or she'd be both stealing and vandalizing. For some criminals, one additional offense was no deterrent but for others, it no doubt was. While Frank opened the padlock, Lee strolled around the area. He imagined Frank up here all alone, focusing only on hitting the targets. It was like putting in golf in most respects. The major difference was the force of the shot. When shooting, you had only to worry if there was adequate force to get a bullet to the target. If it flew beyond the target, that was generally all right. In golf, you had to have enough power to propel the dimpled ball to the hole but you couldn't have excess power either.

Frank had the door opened now. He was doing something inside the shed but from this distance, Lee couldn't tell what it was. No matter. It was certainly an essential task. Frank didn't do things just so he could say he did them. There was a practical purpose for every conscious, and probably most unconscious, act that his friend and coworker performed. Lee's thoughts did a U-turn back to golfing and shooting. There was another interesting comparison between the two activities. Having a really bad day firing a gun could mean you were killed if your target had a gun and had the same goal as you. In golf, constantly missing the target could make one feel like killing themselves.

"You ready for some shootin'?" yelled Frank as he emerged from the cave of the shed, a revolver in each hand.

"Sure. Just as long as the targets can't shoot back," he said.

"You're safe there."

"Good deal."

Frank strode over. He handed Lee one of the guns.

"That's a Colt Mustang .380," he said.

"What's that mean?" he asked.

Frank shot him a look that he wisely chose not to translate into words.

"It means it's a damn gun. Shoot the son of a bitchin' firearm at one of the targets and see if you can hit it."

"Yes sir, Commander Sir. Right away, Sir."

"And I wouldn't be too much of a smartass," Frank began as he started loading cartridges into his gun, "when I'm holding two guns."

"I see your point, Frank. I see it very clearly. So is this loaded?" he asked. Frank nodded.

"Yep. Use two hands. Take aim at a target, relax, and pull the trigger. That's all there is to it. If you miss left, move your aim to the right next time. If you shoot high one time, lower your aim on the next shot. And vice versa. It ain't rocket science, like they say."

"Sure, Frank, whatever you say," he replied and then began selecting a target.

For some reason, he was drawn to the scarecrow. After several seconds of lining up a shot on the figure, he changed his mind. He no longer wanted to shoot at the straw-filled figure. Somehow he didn't feel quite right putting bullets through it. It looked too much like Jesus on the cross. For an instant, a flicker of movement around the scarecrow's eyes, as if they'd magically popped open, seemed to confirm the wisdom of Lee's choice. It was like the Son of God had winked at him. Lee stepped back, shook his head, closed his eyes and then reopened them.

"I'll go for the beer bottles," he finally said.

A grunt of what passed for approval floated over from Frank's direction. Lee zeroed in on the target. He took aim for the one on the far left. He squeezed the trigger, felt the recoil come back for him like an accusation, and waited for the shattering of glass. None was forthcoming, however, as the bullet sailed high and left of the target. Frank was taking aim with his own weapon at a bull's-eye drawn with red chalk on the chalkboard.

Without looking away from his own target, Frank said, "Remember what I said about adjusting your aim. If you miss left, aim more right next time. Miss high, aim lower."

"Got it."

Lee put both hands on the Colt Mustang .380, closed his left eye, took Frank's advice about adjusting his aim, and pulled the trigger. This time he was much closer. The bullet flew only six inches high and a foot left of the Grain Belt bottle on the far left. An explosion from nearby told him Frank had just fired. He glanced over at the chalkboard A hole in the second ring from the middle proclaimed a partial success for his friend. With Frank's experience, nothing short of a bull's-eye would be a total success. But like golf, it frequently took a little while to get warmed up. This was like the tee shot on the first hole. If it went well, that was a bonus. Lee took aim for another shot. This time he decided to aim for the middle two bottles instead of the one on the first one in line. That way he had more room for error. Of course, he'd still need to have the proper vertical placement to hit something. The second bottle from the left shattered.

"All right, come to Daddy!" he shouted.

Frank looked over. He nodded appreciatively, then said, "Good shot, pardner. Now see if you can nail the one on the very left." He returned to his own target shooting.

Without doubting his ability or worrying about failure, Lee knelt down, shut his left eye and took aim. After zeroing in on the target, he squeezed off another shot. The bullet whizzed two inches beneath the plywood supporting the targets. He raised the semiautomatic pistol slight and fired again. This time he was right on. The bullet from the Colt Mustang cut the bottle in nearly symmetrical halves. He'd not only hit the target but had a bull's-eye.

"Hot damn, now this is fun," Lee declared while eyeing the next bottle in line.

"You must be gettin' used to the weight and windage of the Colt. If you get a hankerin' to try another model, let me know. I got a nice Anaconda .44 Mag you could, oh shit, never mind," said Frank.

"What's wrong?"

"I forgot. I left the Anaconda .44 Mag in the glove compartment of my truck. Usually I keep the Heckler & Koch HK-4 in there but I decided I wanted to practice with that one. So I bumped the Heckler & Koch out of the saddle and stuck the Anaconda in its place."

"You keep a firearm in your truck?" Lee began. "Isn't that illegal?"

"Yep. But I figure I'm all right long as I don't get stopped by an officer of the law. That's why I always take 'em out if I'm taking any kind of trip in the truck. But drivin' round Dying Tree is fine. I like to have a revolver nearby just in case trouble comes up in a hurry. Round here, crime ain't exactly runnin' rampant but you never know. All it takes is one troublemaker drunk or stoned on something who suddenly thinks you look just like his daddy who used to knock him around when he was a little boy and now wants revenge or some shit like that. If it's just one guy and he ain't the size of a NFL lineman, I figure I can take him without any guns. But if he's too big and he's got friends to boot, it's good to have a friend you can turn to for help."

Frank sighed and fell silent. It was the just about the longest run of sentences Lee had his friend string together since they'd known each other.

"Does anyone else know about your 'friend'"? he asked Frank.

"Eileen Eide knows. Couple a my buddies from the gun club know. Hell, even old Sheriff McDougal knows. He trusts me. He knows I wouldn't ever use it unless it was a justified case of self-defense."

"I see," Lee said.

He returned to shooting the Grain Belt bottles. This was getting to be almost as much fun as playing golf.

Not quite, but close.

CHAPTER FIFTEEN

Ricky trudged back to his dressing room. They'd just finished shooting the climatic scene from "Massacre on the Prairie". It was the biggest, most complex, expensive, and frustrating scene to shoot. No less than two hundred thirty human actors were involved in the scene. Throw in another thirty-five horses and the number swelled to 265. With all those different people and horses involved, it took fifteen takes before the director was satisfied with it. Ricky's dose of meth had worn off ninety minutes ago. Combined with last night's carousing—Ricky'd stayed out until three o'clock in the morning—the marathon shooting session left the star not just dragging but barely able to function.

He'd just shut and locked his dressing room door when the phone in the living room shrieked at him. Ricky picked up on the third ring.

"Yeah?"

"Ricky, it's Jim Morton."

"Hey Jim. What's goin' on?"

There was an ominous pause.

"Ricky, I've got bad news about the casino project," he spat out. "The other three investors have backed out. You're the only one left and as you know, we can't go through with this without help from other investors. I'm afraid the deal's dead."

"No, that can't be," replied Ricky, nearly yelling.

"It's true. I spoke to Dale Greene today. He said that they had a three-hour-plus conference yesterday. They decided the risk outweighs the potential return on investment. None of them can afford to lose the amount they'd have to invest in the deal. They're essentially rich men right now but their margin of error is still very small. With their personal debt, they can't afford to make a mistake on a major deal like this. If they play it wrong, they're likely to go bankrupt or at least have to give up most of their assets, like their homes, if this goes bad."

"Didn't you convince them the risk is minimal? The casino, bar, and golf course complex would have my name attached to it. People around here would flock to a place like that!"

"Sure, a certain number of people would flock. The key is how many people would flock? You've got your core fans who would gamble there just because you own part of it but how many would continue going after the initial excitement wore off?"

"A helluva lot, god damned it!" Ricky said.

"I think so but the other potential financiers didn't. I'm sorry, Ricky, but the deal isn't going to work out," said Jim.

"No, damn it, it will!" roared Ricky. "I haven't worked this hard to see it end like this. We'll find other investors. It'll just take time."

"But we don't have much time. The Dying Tree Town Council meeting will be next Monday night. That only gives us three and half days to come up with new investors."

There was nothing but silence from the other line. Jim Morton waited for his client to respond.

"There's no need to tell anyone else about this. I know we'll eventually find other investors. It may take a month or two but it'll happen. You just have to keep working your connections on both coasts and somethin'll turn up."

"But what if we don't find replacement investors?" asked Jim.

"We will. Don't sweat it," assured Ricky.

"The government of Dying Tree should know about this development. It's not fair to keep them in the dark about this with the potentially huge amount of money the town may invest in the project."

"Hey, they offered them in the first place. It's not like anyone twisted their fuckin' arm or anything," said Ricky.

"They agreed to finance all those millions with the understanding we would finance the other third. If that changes, it's our moral obligation to inform them," answered Jim.

"No, that's where you're one-hundred percent wrong. The good people of Dying Tree, as represented by the town council, whom were elected by the townspeople, will decide whether or not to help us based on their perception of the project's ultimate success. If we tell them the other potential investors have backed out, their perception will be that the project isn't going to work out," said Ricky.

"That's right," said his agent.

"But who's to say we won't find other investors to replace the chicken shits who backed out? I say we'll find somebody. There's no logical reason to tell the town of Dying Tree about the little setback. We'll just pull ourselves up by the old bootstraps and go on. This thing's gotta work."

"I don't agree. I want to believe it's going work but I just don't know that we can find enough other people with money who believe in it enough to throw in their money. You don't have enough money on your own and even if the city votes for the economic incentives, that won't be nearly enough," said Jim Morton.

"We'll find somebody. With Ricky Mann's name associated with it, it's a can't lose deal!" said Ricky adamantly.

"No, we have to tell the town council and mayor what's going on. Maybe they'll still vote for the deal. Maybe they'll share your viewpoint about it being a sure fire proposition. The point is we have to be honest about it. We're talking about a lot of money here, a lot of money that we didn't earn. These are taxpayer dollars. That represents a lot of hard work by a lot of people. It's our responsibility to put that money to good use."

"Hold on there, Jim. Don't forget who pays most of your salary. It ain't the good people of the Dying Tree. It's yours truly, pardner. Your first priority is always what's best for your client. *Period.* Don't concern yourself with all that high falutin' talk of what's best and right for the people. You just do your job and everything else will take care of itself. In the end, what's best for Ricky Mann is what's best for the people."

"We'll see about that."

"What's that supposed to mean?"

"It means I don't agree with you," began Jim, "and I've got to give this more thought before I decide my course of action. I don't know if I can continue as your agent."

"Well add this to your plate of food for thought: If you don't see the light on your own, I might be forced to play hardball," Ricky said.

"What does that mean?"

Several seconds of silence, then just before Jim was about to repeat the question, the actor said, "Meaning if you quit and tell anyone about our setback with the investors, I will accuse you of embezzling funds. It'll ruin your reputation and even though I might not win the court case, your reputation will be permanently damaged. Findin' other clients will be real hard, maybe even impossible. You just might find yourself lookin' for a new line of work. Odds are real good whatever the new career is, it won't pay as well as the one you've got now. It'd be a real shame it came to that. Course it don't have to come to that. No siree, it surely don't."

"You slimy son of a bitch," growled Jim.

"Now, now, there's no need for abusive language like that, Jim. Come now, we're all civilized adults here, aren't we?" said Ricky, a veneer of exaggerated sweetness sticking to his voice.

"You are really desperate to pad your ego, aren't you? I never thought you'd go this far, Ricky, I really didn't. But I guess it's true what they say about a person's true colors coming out when the going gets tough."

"So are you with me or against me?" asked Ricky. "Trust me, you don't wanna be on the other side of the table from me, Jim old buddy."

"I'm still thinking about it" Jim said before hanging up the phone.

"Well shit, I believe Jimmy's soundin' a mite scared," he said to himself. "He better be scared, damn it. He better be."

CHAPTER SIXTEEN

Eileen Eide sat in front of the personal computer in the den of her home. She shook her head at the rows and columns of figures. She'd prepared the budget for two years from now assuming Ricky Mann's golf course was up and running. After speaking with people in management of other area golf courses, she'd projected a fifteen-percent decline in revenues. That was an optimistic figure, if anything. It might well be closer to twenty percent. But if was fifteen percent, that would mean bad things for her business. She was so highly in debt now that she needed to maintain or improve at least slightly just to keep up with loan and mortgage payments. If revenues from green fees fell off by any more than ten percent, unless she found alternative sources of revenues, Eileen didn't see how she could make it. Her husband had died of colon cancer three years ago. Her two boys, though they earned decent incomes, had so much debt from credit cards and personal loans that they didn't have a dime leftover after paying all their monthly expenses.

Ricky Mann. She'd begun disliking the guy about two years ago. After reading several articles in various entertainment magazines about his extravagant lifestyle and seeing his bar's walls plastered with photos and props from Ricky Mann's movies, Eileen couldn't look at his face without being repulsed with the man's conceit. The whole entertainment industry, which she used to find somewhat fascinating, made her sick. All that ego massaging struck her as a colossal case of waste. Wasted money and wasted time. And of course all the money the stars and their agents and everyone in the movie and TV industry ultimately came from regular people like herself. As long as there were enough regular folks who cared enough to buy videos, pay for tickets to see movies, and so on, the industry would continue on. That's why Eileen decided last year that her New Year's resolution would be giving up movies. She told herself on that fateful New Year's Eve that she'd never again purchase or rent another video from Hollywood nor would she pay to attend movies in theaters. Nearly twenty months later, she'd kept her resolution. For her, there was plenty of drama and themes to be discovered more directly and personally just by paying attention to everyday life.

But now a big-time Hollywood star was threatening to ruin her life and keeping her resolution wouldn't help her. The dirt ball! He'd already made about a hundred times more money than he deserved and then he asks the city of Dying Tree for more money. That took nerve. And the hell of it was there was a good chance the town council would vote to give him the money he was asking for. If that happened, it was a no-win situation. If the project fell flat and Dying Tree failed to recoup its investment, the town was in Grand-Canyon-deep-shit trouble. If the project thrived and the entertainment complex, including of course the golf course, Eileen's business was sunk.

Below the spreadsheet's main body of numbers and labels was a space for comments. Eileen typed in:

SOLUTION TO RICKY MANN PROBLEM: IF COUNCIL VOTES YES ON THE DEAL, THERE IS NO SOLUTION. MAYBE IF RICKY MANN FALLS OFF HIS HORSE AND IS TRAMPLED TO DEATH BEFORE THE VOTE.

"And that's not going to happen, is it?" she sighed.

Eileen saved the file, closed out Excel and exited Windows. She turned off the power on the computer and got up to fix a cup of tea. Though she normally wasn't a drinking woman, she decided a shot or two of bourbon added to the Lipton's sounded like a fine idea.

Damn that Ricky Mann. He'll be the death of me.

* * *

Lee'd recognized Jim Morton's face right away. The memory of their pool match two weeks ago was still fresh in his mind. As Lee drove his utility cart up toward the tee blocks of the seventh hole at the Crazy Horse Golf Club, Jim Morton was pulling a driver out of his bag. Lee threw up a wave as he emptied the garbage receptacle just to the right of the seventh hole. Though it was a bright and beautiful day for golf, Jim's stiff, tense walk and his grave facial expression were darker than Bin Laden's ambitions. Lee had heard on the news that Ricky Mann had issued a dramatic public statement. In it he fired Jim Morton because of embezzlement of over a million dollars. Ricky added that despite the setback, the loss of money wasn't overly serious. Movie deals, product endorsements, and the line of Ricky Mann clothes and toys had provided more than adequate compensation for the star. The announcement shocked the local citizens as well as the entertainment industry. While the Internet and cable channels were abuzz with commentary, rumor and speculation, the subject completely dominated talk in Dying Tree. The editor of the local newspaper, Edward D. Duff, was busy consulting his Hollywood sources for the real scoop. Duff probed his sources for more details. How had the embezzlement scheme been caught? Had charges been filed yet? What was Jim Morton's personal history? Did he have a prior criminal record? Who would replace him as Ricky's agent and financial adviser?

Seeing his face around Dying Tree surprised Lee. He told Jim Morton as much.

"I'm here to try to convince the town council not to vote for the economic incentives," he'd begun explaining to Lee. "You see, Ricky's fellow investors have pulled out. They got cold feet and decided not to risk the money. Ricky didn't want the town council to know because he was afraid they'd vote no on the deal. That's when he devised this scam of accusing me of embezzling a million dollars. It's all a lie but until I can prove otherwise, my credibility is basically zero. Ricky figured no one would believe a crook like me if I said they shouldn't vote yes on the golf course and casino deal. Boy, I'm telling you, he is a devious S.O.B.

"Anyway, I figured it'd be easier to convince the mayor and town council members that Ricky is the liar, not me, if I talked to them in person. Boy was I wrong. Ricky'd already called and spoken to the mayor and three or four of the councilmen over the phone. He made sure he got them on his side before I showed up to plead my case."

"So now what?" Lee asked.

"I don't know. There has to be a way to save the town but I'll be damned if I know what it is. Say, you're pretty new to Dying Tree, right?"

"Right."

"Sometimes an outsider can see things others can't. With me, I've made so many trips to Dying Tree with Ricky that you couldn't rightly call me an outsider anymore. But you, you're acquainted with the town but you haven't lived here long enough to be overly attached to certain ideas. I don't know if it'd solve anything but how about if we meet somewhere private after I'm done with the round? Maybe between the two of us we can come up with a solution. I mean, you seem like someone who cares enough about things like these to do something about it."

"Yeah, sure, I guess so, although I don't know how much of a contribution I'd make," Lee replied. "But if nothing else I'll be a sounding board for your ideas. Maybe just talking about it will inspire an idea you wouldn't have otherwise thought of. Tell you what, I've got one more thing to do after emptying all the garbages around the course. How about if we meet on the practice green at five-thirty? You won't be done much before then anyway."

"Okay but where can we talk in private? I'm not exactly a household face but I've been spotted with Ricky enough times that I'm certain to be recognized if we go to a bar or restaurant. The only people's attention I want to attract right now are the mayor's and town council's. With Ricky's popularity, I'm sure to be in most folks' doghouse. I can do without the media and general public's spotlight right now."

"We'll go to my apartment above the clubhouse," Lee offered.

"All right. Five-thirty it will be."

"See you then."

Lee hopped in the utility cart and made for the eighth-hole garbage.

*　　*　　*

Ninety minutes of brainstorming and bullshitting had produced little in the way of tangible options. Finally Jim Morton gave up. He arose from the kitchen table and thanked Lee for the coffee and his time. The ex-agent extended his hand. Lee shook it.

"It was a good try. Too bad we couldn't have come up with something," Jim said as he turned toward the door.

"What will you do now? I mean, now that you're out of a job," said Lee.

"I have no idea. I'll think of something. I'll survive somehow. I wish I could say the same for this town."

"Well, the town's not dead yet," Lee began. "You know, if this was the Old West, this would be settled with a shootout in Main Street. Ricky Mann and you or some other guy who's handy with a gun, someone like Frank Leeds, would get out the old six-shooters and go to it."

"I didn't know Frank Leeds was good with a gun," Jim said.

"Are you kidding? The guy even carries a revolver in his truck."

"Really?"

Lee regretted saying it the instant after it'd left his mouth but now there wasn't much he could do about it.

"Yep but listen, don't tell anyone else about it. I probably shouldn't have told you."

"Don't worry, your secret is safe with me. But anyway, times have changed since the old days," he said while reaching for the doorknob.

"Not really," Lee said. "Think about it. The main industry here in town is tourism, right?"

Jim's hand rested on the doorknob but he didn't turn it yet.

"Yes. What's that got to do with it?"

"What draws the tourists to Dying Tree in the first place?"

"The myths and legends and heroes of the Old West. Wild Bill Hickok, Wyatt Earp, Doc Holiday, Frontier Bob, Poker-Face Alice, and the general feelings of the time, you know, the exploration of new frontiers, settling of a nation, bravery in the face of great dangers like gun-wielding men with no sense of morals who were completely oblivious to ideas of right and wrong and didn't care a dot for the safety and well-being of their fellow citizens. To put it simply, brave men and women acting to do what's best for the whole community. Whether it was helping a neighbor with farm chores or bringing violent criminals into jail for threatening the general populace, it's the idea of acting truthfully and honestly to help make a little part of the world a better place."

"Right. So the spirit of the Old West is still alive and well in this town, wouldn't you say?" Lee persisted.

"Yes, I guess it is, but again I have to ask, how does that help the situation?"

Lee stared at Jim for a few seconds, then down at the man's feet for a few more, then back up at his face. Finally he said, "That's the thing with spiritual matters. Nothing's set in stone. Everything is fluid, you know, in motion, all the time. There are no hard and fast rules in this area. All I know is that spiritual truths are just as real as any other. A certain female Dying Tree citizen showed me that. The spirit is out there, hell, it's all around us," he said while making a sweeping motion with his left hand. "The trick is tapping into that spirit and acting on it at the right time and in the right place."

"So when and where is that? And through whom is this spirit flowing?" Jim asked before opening the door part way.

"That I don't know . . . yet. I think spiritual phenomena are like quantum physics. It's hard to predict with much accuracy because it's all so fluid. It's chaotic in some ways but in the end, everything works together."

"Right," Jim said, then pulled the door all the way open. "Well, the spirit better get its ass in gear because there's not much time left. Heck, it's possible the council will vote down the deal. Then all this worrying would be for nothing."

"Yeah, that's true, all right. Let's hope that is the case. Maybe we'll get lucky."

"Yes, maybe we will. Well, Mr. Wyatt, I'm off. It was a pleasure knowing you. Best of luck."

"Thanks. And the same to you. I hope everything works out for you. Just keep telling the truth and working hard, and you'll be fine."

"And let the spirits take care of the rest?" asked Jim, a dubious smile accompanying the question.

"Darn right," Lee replied.

Jim smiled, waved, and closed the door. It was a few minutes after seven o'clock. Forsaking home cooking for convenience, Lee decided to order pizza and cheesy breadsticks with garlic dipping sauce from Papa John's. With the night on town with Frank—they'd decided it would be their lucky night so they were going to a casino or two along with their normal list of saloons—slated for tomorrow night, Lee decided that tonight he would spend a quiet evening at home. After the breadsticks, he'd either catch a baseball game on television or read more of the book on eastern religions he'd checked out from the library. If that book failed to keep his interest, he'd turn to "The Complete Guide to Peyote and Other Mystical Drugs," a book he'd purchased through the Amazon web site.

"Papa John's, how can I help you?"

Lee gave the guy his order, got the total, and hung up the phone. He snapped up the book on eastern religions. After reading two pages, he set the book down. Though interesting enough, the passage lacked the ring of truth. Unfortunately he'd left his bible back in Minnesota. Suddenly he sprang out of his seat.

"There's a web site with a complete text of the bible on it. I just need to use one of the library's computers," he said while heading for the front door. After hopping on his bike, he began the short journey to the Dying Tree Public Library. Three minutes later, he remembered his delivery order. Two blocks later, he pulled out his cell phone. He called Papa John's to change the address of the order to the Dying Tree Public Library. The woman sounded confused, hesitated and finally said, "Whatever."

CHAPTER SEVENTEEN

Lee and Frank sat in the Clear Sky Saloon. As for gambling luck, Frank'd been right and Lee had been wrong about their respective fortunes. While his friend hit a jackpot at the quarter machine at Al's Gaming Palace, Lee spent fifteen bucks but won nothing. Lee wanted to go right for the pool tables on the third level but Frank insisted they hit the casino first. He was still riding the wave of good luck, he'd declared confidently. Lee so infrequently saw his friend express joy that he couldn't deny Frank his chance at another jackpot or two. This was prime-time gambling right now. A Saturday night in mid-August meant there were plenty of tourists spending part of their summer vacation here in Dying Tree along with the usual local crowd.

"Well light my cigar with a flame thrower, if it ain't Ricky Mann hisself over thar," drawled Lee in his most satiric imitation of a cowboy yet.

"Well shit in my soup and call them croutons, if you ain't right," Frank shot back.

Lee was dumbfounded. Finally he found voice again.

"My god, Frank, you are in high spirits tonight," he exclaimed.

"Damn straight. I'm tellin' ya, there's somethin' in the air tonight sides just cigarette smoke and cheap perfume," Frank declared and then stuck a dollar bill in the machine.

"Whatever's in the air isn't working for my luck, I can tell you that," Lee griped as he peered at the spinning slots on his friend's machine.

"Oh shit, look at that. The damn thing didn't cooperate with me. Oh well, I got plenty more chances to win," he said. Frank threw in another dollar and pushed the SPIN button. While the wheels spun, Lee threw another glance in Ricky Mann's direction.

The actor was playing poker at his favorite table. Because it was customary for employees and owners of casinos to be prohibited from playing at their own tables, Ricky made the regular dealers give up their job to either a spectator or dealer from one of the competitors. He wanted to erase any doubts about whether the game was honest. Tonight it was Eddie Webster, a dealer from Al's Gaming Palace, who acted on the house's behalf.

"Shit," said Frank before shoving another bill in the slot machine.

Lee returned his attention to Ricky Mann. As usual, there was a good-sized gathering around Ricky. Suddenly a cool breeze blew over Lee's back. He shuddered at its unexpected intensity. Before he knew it, Lee found himself mesmerized by a simple hanging overhead light. It was a plain enough affair, to be sure. Just a white orb but for some reason, it'd drawn Lee's stare. Twenty seconds of intense visual study had been enough to produce an after-image on Lee's retina. The illusion of a purple orb shaped just like the light fixture floated through the air toward him. The purple offspring of the light began revolving as it floated, revealing details of its structure. The minutiae were so intricate, complex and ever changing that Lee couldn't even put a category of shape with them. All he knew was he found it impossible to turn away from it. The first purple, revolving shape blinked out of existence. It was replaced by a second image that acted similarly to its predecessor. The seething, rotating orb was both brilliant in color and fascinating in its movements. Lee watched a third and fourth replica stream toward him. Finally he shook himself out of the trance.

"I'll be right back, Frank. It's getting awfully stuffy in here. Gotta step outside for a minute or two," he said.

"Stuffy? What are you, sick!? It's damn near cold in here with the air-conditioning cranked up like it is," his friend replied before sticking more money into the machine.

"That's what I meant. It's so damn cold in here that I've got to step outside for some warmth."

Frank laughed like a schoolboy fresh out of school for the summer.

"Sometimes you're one weird son of a bitch, you know that?"

"No argument here, old friend. Like Jim Morrison once said, people are strange when you're a stranger."

"Huh?"

"Just keep pumping those bills in. I'll be back before you know it," Lee said as he started for the front door.

"That I can do," Frank replied as he waited for the wheels to stop spinning and give up their secrets.

On his way out, Lee cast another look in Ricky Mann's direction. The movie star wore a smile wider than Lee had ever seen. He wondered if it was because of the card he'd drawn or if he'd heard the rumor about the vote on Monday. While at Al's Gaming Palace, Margaret Chandler, a friend of Frank's, told them she'd spoken with Kristi Martin. Kristi was a friend of hers who worked at the casino where Agatha Hines was gambling tonight. The 80-year-old-retired-schoolteacher-turned-town-council-member had supposedly confided to Kristi Martin that both she and her male friend, Steve McCall, were going to vote yes on the Ricky Mann deal. If it were really true, Ricky had ample reason for the shit-eating grin plastered on his face. That meant the council would vote for the economic giveaways and the town and Ricky Mann would be intimately linked for the foreseeable future.

But it hadn't happened yet. The optical illusion from the light reminded Lee of the evening in the graveyard with Soaring Eagle. He recalled Soaring Eagle's exhortation to focus not on the experience itself but rather on what the experience showed. Instead of concentrating on the wild, fascinating visual and auditory hallucinations, one could achieve illumination and maybe even complete enlightenment by appreciating and understanding what the whole experience, not just the hallucinations, implied. For Lee, the peyote ride was a lesson in the cohesion and unity of all things. Time, space and egos were human constructs that boxed people into corners of categorization. God, the Creator, or whatever term one had for the originator of all sentient beings, was of a completely different structure. Instead of a network of separate, distinct entities, the spiritual plane knew no boundaries. Names and labels, except as road signs pointing toward higher, great truths, were inconsequential.

Lee felt the walls of limitation slowly crumbling as he approached the door, now only ten feet away. Knowing that falling back on past behaviors based on old thought patterns was a delusional trap and projecting possible future consequences would produce only fears of failure, Lee dialed in on the present moment. He trusted his heart to provide the right answer. He didn't know exactly why he had to go outside. Lee simply knew that it was the thing to do. There was an answer waiting out there. His job was to recognize it when he saw it.

*　　*　　*

Jim Morton didn't take the six-twelve flight out of Sioux Falls like he'd planned. He decided to spend the weekend in Dying Tree. He wasn't sure what good he could do but he knew he had to keep trying. Ricky Mann had probably ruined what was left of Jim Morton's life but that didn't mean the now ex-agent was going let the actor ruin the town's life as well.

Because Ricky had declared him a criminal, though no charges had been brought yet, he knew most folks in the town would want to hurt him if they knew he was still in Dying Tree. That concern had prompted him to fashion a disguise for himself. A trip to Wal-Mart, where luckily none of the mostly really young or really old work force or customers, netted him a pair of black cotton jeans, plain black tee shirt, pair of cowboy boots, and wrap-around mirrored sunglasses. One more trip to a western wear shop produced a frilly leather jacket and ten-gallon brown hat. He used cash at both places.

Thusly attired, Ricky Mann's ex-agent approached the Clear Sky Saloon. When he'd gotten to within fifty yards of the place, Jim saw Lee Wyatt push through the doors. He looked strange, almost like he was drugged. That wasn't like him. Jim theorized maybe he'd mistaken drugged for drunk. Maybe old Frank Leeds had bought him a couple of shots of 151 rum or a similar poison. Whatever the reason, Jim hustled over toward him. He'd do whatever he could to help the guy. After all, he'd worked with Jim to devise a solution to the Ricky Mann problem. They couldn't do it but hell, they gave it a shot. You had to like a man like that.

"Whoa pardner, you feelin' okay?" Jim said, the feigned drawl hopefully fooling the dozen or so people milling around the sidewalk who were within earshot. Lee peered at him but with the dark glasses and the rest of the get-up plus the apparently altered state Lee was in, there was no way he'd know who he was.

"Do I know you?" Lee asked.

After Jim had taken five more steps, he said, "Matter a fact, you do."

"All right, I'll bite. Who in the hell are you?"

Jim was now close enough so that no one else around them would hear what he said.

"Yeah, we saw one another on the golf course today. Then we had a little chat afterwards."

"Oh yeah, I know who you are now."

"Say, you feelin' okay?"

"You can drop the drawl, now, by the way. Unless of course you like doing that sort of thing. But anyway, now that I'm outside, I feel fine. Why?" Lee said.

"You looked a little dazed and confused a minute ago. I don't know, your eyes were looking muddled. But now they don't," Jim said truthfully.

"I know why they cleared up. It was because I saw you in this disguise."

"What are you talking about?"

"I got an idea. It may sound kinky because it involves us both being nearly naked for the briefest interval but it's not. Just hear me out first and it'll make sense," Lee said. "But first let's go across the street to the Hitching Post. After we're inside, we'll find ourselves a table."

"You buying?"

"Sure thing, pardner. If you're real good, I might even treat you to a sarsaparilla."

"How could a man turn down an offer like that?"

The two ducked inside.

*　　*　　*

Frank had gotten so into the slots that he'd momentarily forgotten about his friend. He glanced at his watch. Lee'd been gone fifteen minutes. What was he doing outside all this time? Or maybe he'd come back inside the casino and he hadn't seen him. Still, if that were the case, why hadn't come back to see how Frank was doing at the slot machine? Maybe the sly fox had met a woman, thought Frank. Hell, it was possible. Lee wasn't the homeliest man alive and he was an intelligent, intellectual sort. Some women found that attractive, he'd heard. But hell, he still should have told Frank what he was up to. Oh well, Lee acted strange sometimes. He'd come back when he was ready to. Frank almost returned his attention to the one-armed bandit in front of him. However, a flickering overhead light directly above Ricky Mann drew Frank's attention.

It had obviously bothered Ricky. He was said something to the server while pointing at the light. The server, a women in her mid-twenties, nodded and said something to Ricky before hustling over toward the bar area. Probably fetching a maintenance man to replace the problem. Meanwhile the offending bulb continued flashing like a strobe light. Without any conscious awareness on their part, the crowd around the table began slowly disbursing. Though a lot of people still hung around to watch the rest of the hand, they'd left an open path from the table to the front doors. Frank now saw Ricky's cards reflected in the glass frame of the painting behind the actor.

"Well I'll be dipped in shit," Frank whispered when he saw what cards Ricky held.

Then as if on cue, a stranger with a cowboy hat, dark sunglasses, black tee shirt, black jeans, cowboy boots and frilly leather jacket strode toward the table. Frank figured he must have just gotten out of the bathroom. The man, thanks to the crowd's earlier movements, had clear sailing up to Ricky. Suddenly Frank was pulling out a cigarette. Somehow this occasion called for a smoke, though it wasn't exactly an occasion for any reason he could put a name to. Frank flicked a lighter over the tip of the Marlboro 100.

"Ricky Mann," the stranger called out. The famous actor spun around in his chair. He appeared more annoyed than anything else, though Frank thought there was a layer of concern and maybe something even stronger.

"Yeah? Who in the hell are you and what do you want?" Ricky demanded.

"Ain't important who I am. What's important is we got a score to settle," drawled the stranger. "I challenge you to a duel out on main street. Six-guns at ten paces in five minutes. That is, if you got the guts, which I doubt you do."

The casino had, except for the distant din of the incessant music from the various slot machines, fell silent. Ricky peered at the stranger as a huge smile on his face led to a laughter that threatened to double Ricky over with its intensity.

"Good god, now that is the corniest line I ever heard and it wasn't even from a damn movie! I can't believe someone in real life actually said that. Boy, whoever you are, you're a real winner, lemme tell you."

"Mr. Mann, should I take care of this pest for you?" asked Bobby Jorgenson. The director of security at the casino, who sported a short-sleeve flaming red tee-shirt that accentuated his weight-room sculpted arms, had subtly drawn to within ten feet of the poker table where Ricky sat.

"That's all right, Bobby. I'll handle this myself," he said, then turned back to lock eyes with the stranger. "Listen son, I'm busy here. I ain't got time to fuck around with weirdoes like you."

To Frank, from that point on, time slowed down two notches from normal. It was as if a layer of molasses were poured onto the scene.

"So you won't fight me outside?" the stranger asked.

"No. Now get the hell outta here now or I'll run your ass out the front door. You got two seconds to decide if you're goin' on your own or with my boot helpin' your backside through the door."

A few customers chuckled. Frank threw one more look at the cards reflected in the painting at Ricky's back. The problem was Ricky had laid them face down after the mysterious stranger had confronted him. There was no way to confirm, at least not right now, the hand Frank swore he saw reflected in the glass covering the painting of a Native American sitting on his horse overlooking a canyon. But Frank didn't doubt the perceptual ability of his eyes.

"No, now get the hell outta my place or I'll run your sorry ass out the front door myself. You got two seconds to decide if you're gonna walk outta here on your own or if I have to dropkick your sorry ass and the rest of you through the goalposts of life," Ricky said.

Scattered chuckles hang tensely in the air.

"This is your last chance, Ricky Nathaniel Mann. You can fight like a real man or take the cowardly way out. What's it going to be?"

"Listen you fruit-fucking-cake, I said no."

"You'll want to reconsider after I tell you, in private, what I know about the casino deal."

Ricky set his cards down. He studied the stranger from his perch at the card table.

"What the hell are you talking about?"

Lee nodded toward a booth in the far back corner of the bar.

"How about we have a shot or two while discussing this?" Lee said.

Ricky squinted at the booth.

"Deal."

Ricky turned to his main security guy, Bobby Jorgenson.

"Have the bartender deliver a coupla shots, no, make that four shots, of Johnny Walker Blue to that corner table. And make sure no one disturbs us in the next ten minutes."

"Yes sir, Mr. Mann."

Bobby waved down a waitress while Ricky and Lee make their way to the booth. After they're seated, Ricky starts right in.

"Now what in the hell do you know about the casino deal that's so damned important?"

"I know your investor group has backed out and that you haven't found any other takers. The project is doomed to fail. And it'll bring the town of Dying Tree down with it."

"Who in the fuck told you that? Oh hell, I know. You've been talkin' to old Jim Morton, that lyin', embezzling piece of shit. You can't believe a word that guy says."

A waitress swooped in and quietly laid the four shots on the table, two in front of each man. Lee nodded his thanks just before she hustled away from the table.

"Don't try to bullshit me, Ricky. The game's up. I'm onto you. If I had to choose who to believe between you and Jim Morton, and I've got to, I'm going to take Jim's word every time. And a public-smear campaign against me won't work like it did with Jim because I've gotten the would-be investors from the Shearson Group to make a public statement about their decision to back out of the deal if you try any funny business."

Ricky grabbed a shot and threw it back. Lee sipped his while studying the movie star's face. Ricky drummed his fingers on the table while staring past Lee. Lee polished off the rest of his first shot. Ricky snatched his other shot glass and drank it down1. He sighed deeply, closed his eyes and rocked back and forth in chair for a few seconds. His eyes snapped open. He stared down Lee.

"So you're sayin' if I don't shoot it out with you on Main Street that you're going public with this?"

"You got it, pardner."

Lee started in on his other shot.

"And just what the hell do I tell the cops if and when I win the shoot out? It's damn difficult makin' movies and enjoying the fruits of my labors if I'm behind bars."

"You just tell the cops that you were rehearsing for your next movie and that one of the props guys screwed up and gave you a loaded gun. You thought you were firing blanks but tragically, it turned out you were wrong. That's in the off chance you actually win the duel, of course."

Ricky laughed humorlessly.

"You got yourself a deal. So where's my gun?"

Lee unholstered the Glock from Jim Morton and handed it to Ricky.

"I'll meet you outside in ten minutes. I gotta tell Bobby about my supposed shoot out scene rehearsal."

"I'll be waiting. If you're not outside in ten minutes, I'll be coming in looking for you."

*   *   *

An overflowing crowd excited to witness a seemingly impromptu rehearsal for a shoot out scene featuring their favorite movie star packed the sidewalks on both sides of the street. Some onlookers talked into their cell phones while others used them as cameras to take pictures of the event. Ricky and Lee stood twenty yards apart. Ricky has the Glock in his hand while Lee has Franks' .44 Magnum Anaconda holstered on his right side.

"All right Ricky, it's time for one of us to see what the inside of a coffin looks like. We'll draw on the count of three. You ready?"

"It's your funeral, stranger."

Lee nodded while preparing to grab his gun. Ricky does like wise. Many of the bystanders are still on their cells, now giving blow-by-blow descriptions to their listeners. Frank Leeds has a front-row seat. He frowns while scanning the crowd, shakes his head and returns his focus to the duel.

"One, two . . ."

A split second before "three", Ricky grabbed the Glock. As Lee's was still yanking the Anaconda from its holster, Ricky fired. The crowd gasped at the loudness of the supposed blank. An instant later, Ricky's shot buried itself in his target's right thigh. Lee's screamed out, fell to one knee and managed to get off a shot of his own. The bullet pounded into Ricky's chest, blasting the movie star off his feet.

A chorus of murmurs and excited chatter coursed through the crowd. After Ricky Mann failed to move for several seconds, Bobby Jorgenson emerged from the crowd.

"Mr. Mann, hey Ricky, you okay?"

There was no response from Ricky. The director of security rushed toward him.

"Ricky, Ricky, what the hell's goin' on?"

Bobby reached Ricky, saw the actor's lifeless eyes staring into the night sky and knelt in stunned silence by Ricky's body. He turned and peered at the disguised Lee Wyatt.

"You, whoever the fuck you are, just killed Ricky Mann."

Gasps, shrieks and manic murmurings coursed through the stunned crowd. Several people, without being prompted, dialed 911.

CHAPTER EIGHTEEN

All my life I have had an awareness of other times and places. I have been aware of other persons in me . . . You have forgotten much, my reader, and yet, as you read these lines, you remember dimly the hazy vistas of other times and places into which your child eyes peered. They seem dreams to you today. Yet, if they were dreams, dreamed then, whence the substance of them? Our dreams are grotesquely compounded of the things we know.—Beginning of "The Star Rover" by Jack London

Lee Wyatt laid awake in the darkness of his prison cell. He'd occupied this particular rectangle of space in the South Dakota State Penitentiary for two years and two weeks. A jury of three men and nine women deliberated a full ten minutes before forming their verdict. The fact there were hundreds of eyewitnesses to the crime and the public outcry for justice public outcry for justice overrode the defense's contention it was self-defense. A month later, Judge Warner Gerhold, after hearing the prosecutions' and defense's arguments, handed down the death sentence. Death Row in South Dakota was now up to three. A rapist of two teen-age girls and murderer of an elderly paraplegic woman comprised the remainder of the condemned.

Tomorrow evening at six o'clock, right after many folks in the state had finished eating supper, Lee Wyatt would be strapped into the electric chair. With a gallery looking on, he would have electricity passed through his body until dead. Though his parents would be praying for him—his mom told him this repeatedly—they would not be at the execution. Lee didn't blame them. He doubted he could, if he'd had a son or daughter, watch them be executed. Soaring Eagle would be there, though, and that was a great comfort.

One of the many developments his mom informed him of via e-mail (the guards printed out the e-mails from his mother and father and then delivered them to his cell), was the family dog's deteriorating health. The vet found that Casey had severe cataracts. The undyingly loyal, affectionate, upbeat yellow Lab had lost most of his eyesight. In his younger days, a walk in the springtime meant countless tugs on the leash as Casey strained to catch squirrels or robins within visual range. Now walks outside were never more than "potty breaks", as his mom called them. Casey simply couldn't see much more than a foot or two in front of him and though he might occasionally smell a bird or squirrel, his old body wasn't up to even trying to chase them. Mom said if his condition didn't improve, they'd put the animal to sleep. Dad didn't want to talk about it. However, Mom thought there was a good chance they'd bring Casey to the vet for the dog's final shot by week's end.

Which was, if one was talking about the workweek, tomorrow. But Lee didn't want to think about the short-term future right now. The past's nostalgic allure tugged at his mind.

He recalled the visits to his parents' home in Red Wing, MN throughout the last ten years. Whenever Lee and Mary knocked on the front door, two seconds later, they heard the warning bark from Casey. A few seconds after that, just as Lee opened the door to let themselves in, the yellow Lab bounded up to him. After seeing and smelling him, the dog's barks gave way to furious tail wagging and doggy kisses (if Lee bent over to speak to the dog, which he did more often than not). Then Casey would invariably lie between the recliner and wall in the living room as Lee and Mary sat and visited with his folks. At night, the dog, instead of sleeping out in the doghouse or in the breezeway as it did when there was no company, snuggled in and laid at the end of the bed, wedged in-between Lee's feet and the edge of the hideaway bed. It was comforting and soothing to feel the canine's soft fur brushing against the bottoms of his feet as Casey joined them in the land of sleep.

And then there were the long walks around the town parks and through the modest downtown area. Casey seemed to especially relish the walks around Bay Point Park. The park was right next to the river and had several excellent views of Memorial Bluff. For Casey, he got to smell the water and scope out the ducks, geese and terns in and above the brown waters of the Mississippi River. There were the squirrels to consider as well. He was never let off the leash and even if he had, the dog wouldn't have caught them.

However, that didn't stop Casey from exercising his powers of positive mental imagery. Lee was sure that Casey, in the dogs' mental theater, had caught and killed thousands of the gray-furred little shits. Shook the little bastard's scrawny necks until they broke and then snarfed up a squirrel steak complete with absolute no trimmings. Just food, simple, no-nonsense squirrel steak for Casey's imaginary banquets.

Squirrel steak—it's what's for dinner.

"Tomorrow, huh? Don't worry, old partner. God will take care of you," he whispered in the darkness.

"And what about me?" he added.

Lee closed his eyes and tried to sleep. He couldn't relax. Images of the electric chair and his exit from this life set his heart racing and tied invisible cords tightly around his chest. He felt like he was wearing an overly tight straitjacket. Lee leapt up from the cot. He strode over to the iron bars and grabbed one with each hand. The condemned man pressed his unshaven, gaunt face against the cold, hard bars.

"Ahhh," he cooed.

The solidity and coldness cut him loose from the imaginary straitjacket and blew away the death images. But they returned shortly after he turned away from the bars. Knowing he needed to sleep and tired of being battered with the self-imposed barrage of negative energy, Lee forced himself to continue the short walk back to the cot. After lying down, he closed his eyes. Just as he felt the tightness creeping into his chest and the vision of himself strapped into the electric chair, part of a prayer spoken by Jesus crept into his mind. He couldn't recall the chapter and verse from whence it came. All he knew was that he heard it in Sunday school when he was eight or nine back in Minot, North Dakota. After perhaps ten seconds of trying to remember which book of the bible it came from, he gave up. It didn't really matter. All that mattered was that whatever the source, the message found its way through the overrated dimensions of time and space. Softly, in a voice slightly above a whisper, he spoke.

"Know then how to suffer, and thou hast power not to suffer. That which thou knowest not, I Myself will teach thee. I am thy God, not the Betrayer's. I would be kept in time with holy souls. In Me know thou the Word of Wisdom."

After a slight pause, his eyes closed and his hands together, fingertips pointed toward the ceiling and ultimately to the heavens far above, he repeated the first two lines. He paused, breathed deeply, and repeated the same two lines. Soon he didn't have to consciously think about saying the right word at the right time. They began coming out of their own accord, their message and the sound of his voice perfectly unified.

"Know then how to suffer, and thou hast power not to suffer. That which thou knowest not, I Myself will teach thee . . . Know then how to suffer, and thou hast power not to suffer. That which thou knowest not, I Myself will teach thee . . . Know then how to suffer, and thou hast power not to suffer. That which thou knowest not, I Myself will teach thee . . ."

Ten minutes later, the midnight-shift security guard—a plump, earnest man named Mike McDermott—plodded past Lee Wyatt's cell. He frowned. Back in the hallway, not more than a minute ago, when he was just around the corner from where he stood now, Mike McDermott thought he heard a voice coming from the cell. In fact, he was absolutely positive that he had. But now there was nothing. Just the poor condemned bastard snoozing away like he didn't have a care in the world.

That'll change when he wakes up in the morning, he mused while continuing his rounds.

CHAPTER NINETEEN

He couldn't help thinking back to "The Green Mile". The only differences were that he was a skinny white guy with no healing powers and the guy doing the sponge did a thorough job of soaking it in the water. Well, the electric chair was in considerably better shape than Old Sparky was in the movie (and book). But the end result would be the same . . . or would it?

Lee had no illusions about his earthly body ending up as cold and lifeless as Jon Coffey's had been. What he didn't and couldn't fathom was what happened to his seat of consciousness. But that tale was about to be told. Just before they put the black hood over his face, Lee spotted Soaring Eagle in the gallery. She was holding up remarkably well. She wasn't crying but he sensed the tears were about to come onstage any second now.

His mind slipped back to when he began walking, escorted by six security guards, down the hallway leading to this killing place. Unable to keep looking at the looming electric chair, he closed his eyes to the madness. A few seconds after he did, a vision filled his mind. Lee saw himself, his father (Brandon) and Casey on a golf course. While his dad and he bullshitted about various subjects, Casey trotted merrily along. Then halfway down the fairway of the par four hole, Casey trotted off toward a field filled with giant sunflowers and tall reeds. The dog disappeared for a few seconds but then soon resurfaced as it bounded through the towering brush. While Lee and his dad struggled to hit a small, dimpled ball, Casey was having the time of his life. By the time they reached the putting green, Casey, his impromptu romp complete, had returned to his customary spot alongside them.

Then the vision was shattered. One of the guards shoved him into the electric chair and then unlocked the handcuffs from his ankles and wrists. Just as he finished unlocking the last one, another guard began securing the electric chair's restraining devices. Lee swallowed hard and then tried not to look at what they were doing or stare into any of their faces. Soon the guards finished their duty. All but one stepped away. The one, a stocky man with a stubble-strewn face, stared in Lee's direction without looking directly into his eyes.

"Lee Wyatt, you have been found guilty of murder in the first degree of Richard Nathaniel Mann. As required by the laws of the state of South Dakota, you have been sentenced to die in the electric chair. Do you have any final words?"

Lee found Soaring Eagle's face in the crowd, smiled briefly, and said, "This town was under assault just as surely as if it was being attacked by a fleet of tanks. I tried to save the town from being destroyed the best way I knew how. I wish it hadn't reached the desperate point that it did but unfortunately, it did. If given the chance to do it all over again, I wouldn't change a thing. Ricky Mann was an evil, greedy egomaniac—"

A collective gasp erupted from the gallery. Then a wave of a wave of fevered murmurings swept through the room. After they died down. Lee continued.

"Ricky Mann would have destroyed Dying Tree. The only way he could have been stopped was challenging him to a duel and hoping like hell I won. I wish that wasn't the case but since it was, someone had to act. I did and that's why I'm here today. I can live with my actions as I go to the place beyond this life. It is you people here today and folks like you who must live with yourselves and your decision to kill a man. I feel sorrier for you than most of you do for me."

The guard motioned to another guard, a tall, black-haired woman with a bad case of acne. She solemnly approached Lee and proceeded to place the black mask over his head. From the moment the black mask was put on him, Lee lost all sense of time and rationality. On one level, he knew there must have been plenty going on. Guards working mechanisms that turned on the electricity, people in the gallery sobbing, smiling or looking away, the few select reporters straining for the right words to describe the grisly scene, and countless other minutiae.

He knew that but if Lee allowed his mind to perceive the sequence of events, he'd know when to expect the horrible blasts of electricity that would kill him. By shutting off the reactions of the gallery, Lee hoped to distance himself from the physical pain of the execution. And suddenly the pain was upon him. Searing jolts of electricity exacted pain like he didn't know was possible. Part way through the torturous ordeal, Lee felt his consciousness rise above his body. It was decidedly a queer feeling to be gazing down upon his convulsing, dying form. But the vantage point up here was infinitely better than viewing it from his previous position. The only bad part was seeing the reaction of Soaring Eagle. Her head was down as she stared at the floor, the tears now flowing freely.

Lee wondered what his parents were doing right now. He wondered if they regretted not attending the execution. Probably not. What was to be gained by watching their son be killed?

He was going to check out the rest of the killing chamber but couldn't. It had disappeared. All that remained for Lee Wyatt's soul was an unending field of blackness. Into this limitless void he traveled, conscious thought a luxury or curse he would no longer harbor. Some unknowable time later, Lee found himself walking up stairs that had been carved into the side of a mountain. Squinting into the cloudless sky, he was unable to see where the mountain ended. Lacking a better plan, he kept climbing.

The trail he traveled by foot was like a mountain road with a series of switchbacks. He'd just rounded yet another corner when a yellow Lab jogged up to him. The canine sat and stared up at him. It looked like Casey did when he was a young adult dog. Just beyond puppydom but not quite at adulthood. The teen-age of dogs, Lee thought.

"Hi boy."

The dog's tail began wagging a hundred and eighty miles an hour, the lab's eyes bright, alert and completely focused on him. Lee's spirit-body bent down and gently patted the dog's head.

"Well, I'm going to keep walking upward. You're welcome to join me."

The dog responded by following at Lee's heels as he continued the trek up the side of the mountain. Sometime later, Lee felt a queer sensation. His point-of-view shifted abruptly. Now he was seeing this world, whatever world it truly was, from a decidedly lower perspective. Moreover, now he could view what used to be "his" body walking ahead of him.

Good Lord, I've switched places with the dog.

And so he had. Lee, now a dog, continued up the mountain-side trail. Any memories of his previous life had disappeared like smoke. All he thought about now was the path in front of him. Then after a series of switchbacks (he knew not how many as dogs cannot count), Lee-the-dog spirit witnessed the human ahead of him speaking with another human. The human—a man—wore a red-and-white checkered flannel shirt, tan, leather ten-gallon hat, and dirty blue jeans. Though the dog couldn't speak their language, he could understand it.

"Good to see yah again," the stranger said, a cigarette dangling between his lips.

The man named Lee frowned.

"Again? Have we met before?"

The stranger smiled, drew in a deep toke from the cigarette, and blew out a stream of white smoke.

"That's right, you folks tend to forget."

"What do you mean, *you folks?*"

He shrugged, and then said, "Just folks who've gone away for a time, gone down a level. People like that got real short-term memories 'bout the real important, powerful stuff. Easy to get caught up in all that glittery, superficial razzamatazz down there. Guess I was that way once upon a time myself. Yah lose your priorities when yer away from here for too long."

"What is this place? Is it heaven?" the human with Lee Wyatt's body asked, Lee's spirit observing and listening closely from his new four-legged, canine perspective.

The old cowboy, deep-set wrinkles, like crevices on the moon, covered most of his face. He toked the cigarette briefly, grimaced and then blew out another stream of smoke.

"Does it feel like heaven?"

Lee's old body shrugged, and then said, "Not exactly as I'd envisioned it but who knows what heaven really looks like? I mean, unless you've been there."

The cowboy belted out gales of laughter, which quickly devolved into fits of coughing. Eventually he regained his breath as the laughter and coughs subsided.

"That's the heck of it, partner. You've been there but you forgot all about it. This here place, well, you'll see what it's all about for yerself, which is the only way you ever learn anything important, I reckon."

Lee, in the dog's body, found him/itself nodding. The old cowpoke, whatever or whoever the hell he was, seemed to have a grasp of the really big truths in life. He took one more drag off the butt before putting the thing out by pressing it into the palm of his hand. He didn't flinch an iota. The old cowboy laughed and shook his head.

"Still have a hard time gettin' used to that."

He waved as he turned and then proceeded to stride right toward the edge of the drop off. As there was for most of the rest of the mountain trail, a four-foot-high wall of brick acted as a safety guard. He hopped it on it, stared down, and closed his eyes tightly.

Suddenly the old cowboy's human form had transformed itself into a bald eagle. The creature, wings furiously flapping, cast one last glance back at the human and canine forms. Lee stuck up his right front paw as the bald eagle flew away. Lee's old body was already walking up the mountain path. He/it trotted to catch up with his old human form. Up the side of the mountain they trekked. Lee the dog kept waiting for a dramatic change in scenery or another encounter with spirit-bodies like the cowboy they had just met. His expectations were not fulfilled, however. Repeated glances upward failed to reveal where the mountain ended.

The twin transformations were so gradual that Lee now could not pinpoint when they occurred. All he knew was that now instead of occupying the dog's body, his spirit was back in his old spirit-body and instead of climbing upward toward a distant peak, he and the dog were traveling horizontally across a vast expanse of desert. Boulder-sized tumbleweeds blew across their path a couple times while two- and three-story cactuses stood in scattered spots throughout the landscape. Though he knew he shouldn't be, years of conditioning had taken their toll. Lee still felts occasional stabs of hunger and thirst. Eventually, after what could have hours or weeks—the incessant, crushing hand of time was itself crushed now that Lee was free of his physical vessel—the need for material sustenance melted away. He glanced down at the young yellow Labrador. It looked back at him and said, in canine language, "What?" or maybe, "Yes?"

"Just seeing how you were doing, that's all."

They kept walking. Up ahead, Lee saw the landscape was different. Instead of the tan sand background splashed with cactus-green and tumbleweed-spheres, a brilliant blue body of water stretched on for an indeterminate distance. Figures, apparently human, moved around the shoreline.

"Now we're getting somewhere," remarked Lee as he looked down at the dog. "But I wish we could get there faster."

The yellow Lab winked at him. The dog then stopped, sat down on its haunches, and closed its eyes. Within five seconds, the dog had shed its former form. It was now a giant cheetah. In fact, it was so big that the cat had to lie down on its stomach so Lee could climb on its back. The instant Lee climbed aboard, the tank-sized cheetah blasted off. Lee lunged and dug his fingers into the cat's fur on the sides of its neck so he wouldn't be thrown off. With his hair blowing back and heart racing, he rode the racing animal toward the water.

When they were a hundred yards away, the big cat slowed down to a trot. At fifty yards, it slowed to a walk. Lee hopped off and began walking on his own. He was entranced with the dancing figures just beyond the reach of the waves. Though Lee saw a few human figures—two black men and one Asian woman—the majority of the figures were animals. Polar bears, black bears, kangaroos, cows, and wolves comprised most of the group. Thirty to fifty yards above the dancing masses, a variety of birds—mostly terns and sparrows with a smattering of cardinals and robins—flew in synch with the movements on the ground.

Lee glanced over at his animal companion. He was back to his old doggy self. The canine trotted happily along at his side. The two approached the dancing hordes. A bunch of bears moved aside to allow them passage to the bridge that had magically appeared. Shooting from the main bridge were countless other bridges of varying size, color and material. Rust, chocolate brown, jet black, purple polka-dot, piss yellow, midnight blue structures of iron, steel, wood and aluminum shot off in various directions. The only consistency was variation.

Moreover the bridges all ended at mini-islands with different players on the islands. Lawyers, accountants, and computer network analysts mixed in with mail carriers, bricklayers, and ditch-diggers. Mothers of three and four were shown alongside fifty- or sixty-plus-year-old bachelors. Saints were neighbors with pedophiles. White-tailed deer and hunters with fluorescent-orange clothes took up residence by one another. Mourners listening to 21-gun salutes and prayers for the dearly departed stood by maternity wards brimming with babies and new life.

And the islands continued on, on both the left and right, for as far as Lee could see. The variety of life and seething energy was driving him nearly crazy.

"Just chill, all right," he told himself. "Keep moving straight ahead and all will be fine." He turned to the dog. "Isn't that right?"

The dog ignored him. It was too busy scoping out the islands on the right side.

"Fine then. So much for man's best friend."

They continued on. The day faded to twilight and then night. Still they were walking, both sides of the bridge populated with islands featuring human beings (and occasionally animals) in some life situation.

Though time was no longer a consideration, it seemed to Lee like they'd walked, after nighttime arrived, another five or six hours. Whatever the distance and numbers, Lee's mind was nearly asleep. Suddenly he felt the bridge underneath them vibrating wildly. He glanced to the right. All the islands and their connecting bridges were skimming across the black water to take up positions just ahead of him and the dog. From God-knew-how-many miles back, all the countless islands and the inhabitants repositioned themselves. Instead of lining up in a straight line, presumably because of the sheer numbers, they formed a giant circle.

After all the island residents had positioned themselves, Lee began walking around. Because the islands had reformed in addition to the people and animals, now there was a vast circle of solid ground. It was upon this giant circle of sand that Lee Wyatt and his canine companion traversed. At each station around the circle, the residents waved, smiled or made some kind of friendly, well-meaning gesture. They were about a quarter-way around when Lee halted. The dog followed suit.

The inhabitants at this station weren't merely smiling or waving like the other ones. On this station, all the residents were in action. A man and woman, each appeared to be in their late 30's, were out for a walk through a sprawling city park. The man, a skinny guy with a slight paunch and receding hairline, pushed a stroller with two smiling babies in it. The woman, a stocky blonde with wide hips, kept two Rat Terriers in line with retractable leashes. Barking, romping, jumping, and sprinting, the two little dogs were having the times of their lives. Their owners smiled brightly at the dogs' antics. Even the babies laughed at the canines.

Lee was drawn into the middle of the scene. At first, he was an elm tree, then the rushing stream and finally the baby stroller. He studied the Rat Terriers. They literally launched themselves for jumps. After watching the tri-colored dogs jump several times, Lee was able to merge his spirit with the slightly larger Rat Terrier. Now he was bouncing crazily off the ground, reeds and sunflowers and trees towering above him. Ten or twelve steps later, he flew into the air, his little puppy body sailing through space toward the raging creek down below. The dog landed five feet short of the creek but the experience left him breathless. His doggie-friend trotted back toward the path where his owners and brother dog were.

Lee was about to wonder what this was all about when but then suddenly lost all conscious thought. Though he felt himself breaking up, Lee could do nothing about it. Now he was back inside the giant circle. The sky was moonless. The few stars he saw cast a milky light that failed to illuminate the vast field of darkness in which he stood. Though he couldn't see all the spirit-bodies around him, he knew they were there. Their energy was palpable. In addition, Lee heard the sporadic rustling and shuffling sounds. He wondered what was next. Was he supposed to say something? Do something? Was there a ritual in the afterlife one was supposed to know? If so, he wasn't one of the ones in the know.

o he waited.

nd the dog waited.

ind they waited.

ee was about to lay down with his chin on the ground like the dog
n a glimmer of light appeared fifteen feet in front of him. The dog and
oth perked up, though he didn't cock his head like his canine friend.

sliver of golden light widened and sprouted upward. As the shape grew
volume, it grew more defined. It was a male with a brown beard.

Jesus.

Lee could tell it was Jesus more so from the aura of sheer love and
ntleness washing over him than by the outward appearance. Then from
rectly behind Jesus an oriental man's face appeared.

Buddha.

The Buddha's face dissolved, the millions of tiny face-fragments flowing
nto the body of Jesus. Jesus stood and smiled at him. Then he looked down
it the dog. The Son of God wore a simple white robe and leather sandals.
The most remarkable piece of clothing was the multicolored cape. Upon
closer inspection, Lee saw that different colors in the cape weren't normal
fabric. There were tiny faces and figures, mostly human but perhaps a third
of them recognizably some form of wildlife.

"Peace be with you, my son," said Jesus.

Lee was speechless for several seconds. Finally he stammered, "Thank
you. Peace be with you."

"You know, most convicted killers do not make it up here."

"I don't doubt the truth of that but in my case, there were extraordinary
circumstances."

Christ smiled and said, "Indeed they were, my son."

"I did what I thought had to be done to save the town from ruin," Lee
said.

"And the legal system did what they thought they must to carry out
justice."

"They did."

"And so that is why we have the pleasure of meeting this night," Christ
said.

"Yes, Holy Father, that's exactly right," Lee, said. "So where do we go
from here?"

"That is up to you, ultimately. But before you decide anything, there
is something I must do. Come closer," Jesus said while motioning with his
right hand.

Lee slowly walked toward the caped, smiling figure. When he'd drawn to within a foot, Jesus reached out with his right hand and placed it gently on top of Lee's head. He almost fell back as the flow of love and compassion and divine power pouring from the hand and dispatched waves of warmth all through Lee's soul.

"In name of the Father and the Holy Spirit, and on behalf of the Father and the Holy Spirit, I grant you the complete forgiveness of all your sins."

The words sent even more warmth cascading over his spirit-body. Because it was a holy event, Lee had had his eyes closed for the last several seconds. When he finally opened them, Jesus' right hand was still atop his head. The rest of the landscape had changed dramatically. The immense field of blackness had been transformed. Now all the beings who'd formed the giant circle around him were ablaze with luminescent blue light. Their faces and bodies, though all slightly different, glowed with a startlingly blue shade, even more dazzling than the blue of the Aegean Sea around Greece and Turkey. A thin ribbon of golden light, like the color of the rising sun, flowed from and through each of the blue bodies. Looking down at his own body, Lee saw the same golden light flowing from himself to Jesus. The light was so bright that it was difficult to clearly see Christ's expression. Lee sensed more than saw Jesus.

"It is important that you not let your decision on your future be marred by guilt over past sins. You must not retain your sins, lest they poison your mind and cloud your judgment. You are now free to go where you think you must, do what you believe is the best for mankind, and become the type of soul you were meant to be."

Jesus withdrew his right hand from the top of Lee's head. He grasped Lee around his shoulders. Then all the separate spirit-bodies in the vast circle began flying toward them. Lee watched as the countless blue orbs entered into the cape on the Son of God's back. As each blue orb was absorbed into the cape, it immediately changed to a different color, each one a unique design. As Lee watched the shapes enter the cape and then move about in dancing-like motions, he heard his canine friend whimpering from behind him.

"It is all right, little one," Jesus began, "come here. I will not harm you."

More whimpering and then a growl. Lee was more focused on the dancing colors in the cape. A glance around revealed an unbroken field of white light surrounded them. There was no form anywhere except for himself, the yellow Lab and Jesus. And of course, the cape.

"There, you see. It is all right," Lee heard Jesus say to the dog.

He felt the soothing security of the dog's spirit-body brush up against him. Still, he couldn't take his eyes off the cape. It seemed to have grown a hundredfold in the last minute or so. Each of the thousands of different specks of life had so many dimensions and depth to them. It was difficult deciding where to focus his attention. So many possibilities, so much life and love and energy emanating from the cape.

"Peace be with you, gentle one," he heard Jesus tell the dog. Jesus said something else but he didn't hear it. Couldn't hear it, really, because his soul was already traveling away from the Lord. It was difficult leaving but as Jesus said, the Father and He would be with him always. Toward the cape he flowed. As the cape grew larger, Lee finally decided what part of the cavernous space he wished to go. As he neared the gyrating, restless ocean of movement, he felt what little emotional and psychological baggage he carried drift away into the chasm of forgetfulness. By the time he reached the niche in the cape that caught his spiritual eye, Lee forgot he was ever known as Lee.

Somewhere behind him, as if through a long tunnel, he heard a dog barking. The woofs echoed for a long time. And then they were gone.

*   *   *

Soaring Eagle zipped along in her blue Talon. She was en-route to the sacred peyote ceremony. She and seven or eight others were to gather at Carlos Sabina's countryside mansion with the ritual to begin at seven o'clock sharp. It was 6:15 p.m. now. If she drove the speed limit, she'd be there in a half-hour. Soaring Eagle was almost out of Dying Tree's city limits when she hit the brakes hard. She slowed down just enough to screech out a right-hand turn onto Maple Street.

"Gotta get water," she said to herself. Two blocks ahead on the right was a Holiday store.

A block later, as the car eased to a halt at a red traffic light, Soaring Eagle frowned at the animal shelter on her immediate right. For some reason, she felt an incredible urge to zip in and see what kinds of animals were available for adoption. She shook her head, blinked her eyes several times and thrust her eyes back on the road in front of her.

"Remember what you came for. Get the water."

She didn't want to be late for the ceremony. Carlos and the others did not appreciate late arrivals. The practitioners' time was valuable and everyone respected that, though their very beliefs somewhat mitigated the lateness factor. Unlike most of the rest of society, they appreciated and occasionally perceived the timelessness and eternal nature of God. But despite that, tardiness was a sign of disrespect for the Creator. She was always punctual for the communion ceremonies. Tonight would be no exception.

The light was green. Soaring Eagle gunned the Blue Talon through the intersection. She could see the red, white and blue Holiday sign growing larger by the second.

*   *   *

Harriet Dvorak saw by the reading in the lower right-hand corner of her computer monitor that it was 6:20. Only ten minutes left before her work day here at the New Hope Animal Shelter was done. She glanced over at the front cages. Though most of the cages were located in back, out of sight from most of the staff and visitors to the shelter, a shortage had forced the center to install ten additional cages. They completed the installation almost six months ago but Harriet still wasn't used to it. It wasn't so bad if the ones in the front cages were adopted. When they weren't, it gave her a serious case of the guilts.

Max, a combination Portuguese Water Dog and Cocker Spaniel, had been with them for two months. Three families thought about adopting him. However, after hearing he was prone to nipping or even biting children, they ended up choosing a different dog. Though the shelter's policy wasn't etched in stone like the laws Moses brought back, there wasn't a lot of leeway. If after two months an animal was not adopted, euthanasia was the logical next step. After all, the New Hope Animal Shelter could house an orphan dog or cat (or whatever) for only so long. The occupancy rate for the area shelters, just like the prisons for humans, was high, pushing 100% in many cases.

Harriet had managed to insulate herself from emotional attachment simply by limiting her looks in the direction of the cages and using the animal's names as little as possible. Instead she used the control or case number assigned to them. With Max, it was different. Maybe because Harriet knew right from the start Max was a goner. Biters were much like the cockroaches in the old TV commercials. They checked in but they didn't check out. Well, in a manner of speaking, they really did check out. They checked out to go to that big doggie house in the sky.

Harriet cast a rueful look in Max's direction. The dog was medium-sized, around forty pounds, with predominantly black fur, alert brown eyes, and a smattering of white on its chest. Max barked more than most of the other dogs, occasionally even howling. Today he'd been silent save for a short bout of whimpering in mid-morning and a bark of excitement when he saw his supper being brought toward his cage.

"Well old friend, we tried to find you a home, we really did," she told the dog. Max, even though Harriet hadn't used his name, stared intently through the wire mesh of the cage. "Well, at least he's got the weekend," then added in little more than a whisper, "as much good as that'll do him."

It was six twenty-five. Harriet began shutting down her computer.

*   *   *

Soaring Eagle was buzzing back down Maple Street toward Main Street. While approaching the traffic light, she was prepared to gun it if need be in order to make it through. The message DON'T WALK began the telltale flashing. It'd be turning yellow in a second or two. She pressed hard on the Talon's accelerator. Forty yards away from the intersection, Soaring Eagle noted there was no traffic coming from the opposite direction. Although she hadn't planned to, she found her left hand flicking on her left turning signal.

After slowing down to fifteen mph, she executed a left turn onto 2nd Street. Before she could find a good reason not to, Soaring Eagle found herself turning right into the parking lot of the New Hope Animal Shelter. The clock on her dashboard flashed 6:26. As Soaring Eagle stepped toward the front entrance, she saw they closed at 6:30.

"Get your butt moving," she admonished herself just before pulling open the glass door.

A short woman with a tan face and curly white and black hair smiled from behind the front desk.

"May I help you?"

Soaring Eagle stared dumbly back, searching for an answer.

"I, I, ah, I'd like to adopt a pet. A dog, actually," she found herself saying.

"We're supposed to be closing in just a few minutes. Can you come back tomorrow?" the woman asked.

"Please, this won't take long. I'll know the right one when I see it. I won't take up much of your time," Soaring Eagle said.

"What breeds appeal to you?" the animal shelter employee—Soaring Eagle noticed an ID badge stuck on the woman's chest that read HARRIET—asked her.

All she could do was shrug her shoulders and smile sheepishly. Harriet sighed and shook her head in disgust. Her irritation evaporated in the blink of an eye. Now she smiled brightly at Soaring Eagle.

"Well, if you don't have any particular breed of dog in mind, I've got a special little guy I think you should meet. Come right over here," Harriet said while marching over toward Max.

After they were about ten feet away, Max hopped up from his slumber, his cropped tail zipping back and forth like insults between guests on the "Jerry Springer Show".

Harriet bit her tongue. In her mind, she was saying, He's got about two days to live and he tries to take hunks of children's faces. Okay, maybe they were both slight exaggerations of the truth but only slight. If Max was still haunting this building come Monday, Harriet didn't like his chances of seeing another weekend. And who knows, if Max would have hit his target instead of chomping on thin air, he would probably would have tore some skin on those kids.

"That's Max. He's been at the shelter for just over two months. Has a tendency to nip, especially children," she finally said.

Soaring Eagle nodded thoughtfully. Then she knelt down and pressed her face within an inch of the cage. Harriet, though hopeful, felt a knot of fear form in her stomach. Max couldn't do any harm right now but if he lunged, it'd probably scare the hell out of this poor woman.

And seal the dog's own fate.

Max's tail continued wagging frenetically, the canine's jaws hanging open as it peered back at the kneeling woman.

"By the way, what is your name? Even if you don't end up with an animal, I'll need it for the log sheet."

"Soaring Eagle."

"That's poetic."

"Thank you. Whenever I'm sad or depressed, I remember my name. It reminds me that spirits should always soar through the skies of hope like the eagle. Most people think it is corny but traditions mean more than what anyone else outside the tribe thinks."

She refocused her attention on the caged canine.

"Can we let him out?" she asked. "I want to pet him."

"Are you sure? I mean, I can do it but first I gotta lock the front doors. We are officially closed anyway. I'll be right back."

Harriet hustled over to lock up. After withdrawing the key from the lock, she wheeled and rejoined Soaring Eagle and Max.

"So you want to meet Max close-up and personal, huh?"

"Yes."

"Okay, just don't make any quick movements, especially with your hands, that he might misinterpret."

"All right."

Harriet picked through the keys on her ring set until finding the correct one. She inserted the key, turned left and slowly pulled the cage door back. Max glanced at her for a split-second, then stepped through the opening. Soaring Eagle stepped back to give the dog a little space. Then she sat down right in front of Max, her bottom plopped down on the cold, hard tile floor. She leaned over a few inches so that her nose and Max's snout were only several inches apart.

Oh shit, and there's no vet on duty anymore.

"Remember what I said about nipping," she said quietly but forcefully.

"I do."

Soaring Eagle peered into the dog's brown eyes. Max, who'd been on all fours, sat on his haunches.

"Max, do you want to come home with me?" she asked.

The black and white canine looked briefly in Harriet's direction as if soliciting advice on how to answer the question. He turned his gaze back onto the female seated in front of him. Perhaps five seconds later, with Harriet almost cringing with fear for Soaring Eagle and for her own ass if he bit her and drew blood, Max did move.

"You can shake?!" exclaimed Soaring Eagle. She grabbed the dog's paw and they shook.

"Good dog! Max, I am happy to meet you too. My name is Soaring Eagle." Then, to Harriet, she said, "Bring on the paperwork and tell me how much to make the check out for. Max is coming home with me." Then to Max, "Isn't that right, partner?"

The canine stared back and smiled.

"Actually Max, I'm going to rename you. From this point on, you're going to be known as Wyatt Lee. How does that sound?"

The dog cocked its head, peered at Soaring Eagle. Then the dog turned to gaze at Harriet, who smiled and shrugged.

"I think it's got a nice ring to it."

The dog turned back to Soaring Eagle. It slowly brought its right paw up, as if waving at his new owner.

"I believe that is, in canine speak, a resounding yes."

Printed in the United States
154333LV00002B/48/P

9 781441 523211